CAMPFIRE STORIES
FOR KIDS

A STORY COLLECTION OF URBAN LEGENDS, HUMOROUS AND SCARY STORIES, REAL LIFE ADVENTURES AND CAMP FIRE TALES TO MAKE YOU JUMP!

DRAKE QUINN

Disclaimer:

These stories and characters are totally fictitious. Names, characters, businesses, places, events, locales, and incidents are either the products of the author's imagination or used in a fictitious manner. Any resemblance to actual persons, living or dead, or actual events is purely coincidental.

This book is presented solely for entertainment purposes. Do not attempt to try anything you read in this book at home.

This collection includes two tales based on true stories. Lost in Yellowstone, is based on a story of Truman Everts, who was lost in Yellowstone National Park for 37 days. The Legend of Tsali, is based on true events that took place in the year 1838.

We must go beyond textbooks, go out into the bypaths and untrodden depths of the wilderness and travel and explore and tell the world the glories of our journey.

JOHN HOPE FRANKLIN

INTRODUCTION

Are you looking for stories to tell around the campfire? Maybe you want to relive marvellous memories of magical nights camping out?

If you love listening to stories with a twist in the tale or a surprise ending, you're in the right place. We've created this camp fire story collection just for you.

There's stories about farts and boogers, and tales of cowboys and graveyards.

There's spooky ghost stories and scary tales to make your hair stand on end.

There's some funny tales that'll make you laugh or jump out of your skin.

There's stories of graveyards and screaming, there's tales of native Americans, Bigfoot and fire gods.

And there's a couple of stories with corny jokes that'll probably make you groan.

We strongly recommend asking a parent or guardian to read or listen to them first. We accept no liability for any reader or listener who might have nightmares after hearing these spooky tales.

Enter and listen at your own risk!

Let's start with a spooky ghost story, are you ready? Then let's begin ...

ONE

THE GHOST OF THE BLOODY FINGER

"Quit pushing me around," shouted Addie at her big brother, Ben.

She was fed up that she always got told what to do by Ben and Emily, just because they were older than she was.

This time Ben was trying to 'borrow' Ted, Addie's teddy, for an experiment he was carrying out in the garden.

"You can't have him and you can't make me!" Addie exclaimed.

She'd seen what happened before when Ben 'borrowed' her stuff - sometimes it came back broken, but mostly it just didn't come back at all.

There was no way she was going to let Ben take Ted away from her. Ted had been there for her, when Ben and Emily were being mean to her. He'd been there to hold on scary dark nights, when she'd felt afraid. Ted went everywhere with her and she wasn't going to give him up without a fight.

"Come on Ad, it'll be alright, you'll see," insisted Ben.

"No way, I'd rather go inside the old mansion on Halloween than give up Ted!"

"You would, would you? We'll see about that," said Ben.

Then he called out to his sister who was watching TV in the next room, "Emily, you've got to hear what Addie's just said, you'll never believe it!"

"What now?" asked Emily.

"Addie says she's not afraid to go up to the old mansion at Halloween."

"Ha! That's something I'd love to see," said Emily. "Little Addie who can't even get to sleep without Ted by her side, going up to the old mansion on the scariest night of the year."

"Not just going up to, but going in to," said Ben.

"No way! That's never going to happen," said Emily.

"So much for sisterly love and support," thought Addie.

Addie looked her sister in the eye. "I could do it, I don't believe that what they say about it is true."

"So, you don't believe in the ghost?" asked Emily.

"There's no such thing as ghosts, but even if the stories are true, I wouldn't be afraid," replied Addie.

"Not even a ghost which people have been telling scary stories about for years and years?" said Emily. "I heard that even Big Billy Blackridge ran away from that house after hearing the sound of the ghost moaning."

"Quit being so silly. I'm not a scaredy cat and I'll prove it to you!" said Addie, sounding rather more confident than she felt.

"OK then," said Emily, "Halloween night is right around the corner. You'll soon get your chance to prove it."

"Let's all go. We can take turns. Then we'll see who's really a scaredy cat," replied Addie.

"Alright Shrimp," said Ben. He was using the nickname he often called her. She hated it. Just because she was the youngest, they thought she didn't count. She knew she was just as brave and strong as they were, even if she wasn't quite as big.

"I'll show them," she thought to herself.

"You're on, but not a word to anyone about this. It'll be our secret."

A few days later, after dark on Halloween night, Ben, Emily and Addie crept through the rusty gates and were sneaking up the driveway to the old mansion.

"Do you think anyone actually lives here?" whispered Emily.

"Who'd be brave enough to live in the same house as a ghost?" Ben replied, in a hushed voice.

"Ben, you go first,' said Addie.

Ben was the oldest, so he took the first turn.

Emily and Addie hid themselves behind a bush, whilst Ben crept forwards towards the mansion.

Ben tiptoed up the creaking steps towards the front door.

Spying an open window, he crept over the ledge, with its flaking paint.

Soon, he was inside the mansion. Looking around him, through the blackness, he could see furniture covered with dust sheets and thick cobwebs hanging down from a chandelier.

"I hope this is as scary as it gets," he thought to himself.

Stepping as slowly and quietly as he dared, he moved silently across the room to the door on the other side.

As he turned the handle, it gave a loud creak, which seemed to echo through the whole house.

As he opened the door, he heard a sound coming from the floor above.

Clear as day, he heard someone moaning and saying these words, "I am the ghost of the bloody finger. I am in the upstairs bedroom."

Ben didn't wait to find out where the voice came from. He turned around and ran. He ran back across the room with the cobwebs hanging from the chandelier, he jumped through the window with paint peeling on the sash, he ran down the creaky steps leading away from the front door.

When he got to the bush where Emily and Addie were hiding, he was panting and out of breath from running.

"Don't go in there," he said, "I heard it, there really is a ghost."

"Quit your moaning," said Addie. "I don't believe you. You're just trying to scare us! Emmy, it's your turn."

Emily felt rather curious. If there was a ghost, she wanted to see it.

"I'm not going to miss out on my turn," she said, "I want to see for myself."

Emily crept up the creaking stairs towards the front door.

She crept over the window ledge, with its flaking paint.

Around her, through the darkness, she could see furniture covered with dust sheets and thick cobwebs hanging down from a chandelier.

"Nothing scary so far," she thought to herself.

Slowly, quietly, she moved across the room to the door on the other side.

As she turned the door handle, it gave a loud creak, which seemed to echo through the whole house.

Slowly, deliberately, she opened the door, the creaking sound only grew louder.

Then, clear as day, she heard someone moaning and saying these words, "I am the ghost of the bloody finger. I am in the upstairs bedroom."

4

Emily didn't wait to find out where the voice came from. She turned and ran. She ran back across the room with the cobwebs hanging from the chandelier, she jumped through the window with paint peeling on the sash and ran down the creaky steps leading away from the front door.

She arrived back at the bush where Ben and Addie were hiding, breathless and afraid.

"I heard it too," she said, "there really is a ghost. Come on, let's get out of here!"

"Quit your moaning, it's my turn and you're not going to scare me out of it," said Addie.

"Good luck Shrimp," whispered Ben.

She set off and strode up to the old mansion. She crept up the creaking steps towards the front door.

She climbed over the ledge and through the window, with it's flaking paint.

She looked around the gloomy room with its furniture covered with dust sheets and thick cobwebs hanging down from the chandelier.

"I ain't afraid of nothing and there's nothing to be afraid of," she thought to herself.

Silently, she moved across the room to the door on the other side.

As she turned the door handle, it gave a loud creak, which echoed through the whole house.

As she opened the door, the creaking sound grew louder.

Then, clear as day, she heard someone moaning and speaking these words, "I am the ghost of the bloody finger. I am in the upstairs bedroom."

But Addie was not going to be so easily frightened. She kept moving, walking slowly across the hallway to the bottom of the stairs.

Again she heard the voice moaning, "I am the ghost of the bloody finger. I am in the upstairs bedroom."

Addie took one step, then another, up the wide, winding staircase. Finally she reached the landing.

Again, the voice moaned loudly, "I am the ghost of the bloody finger. I am in the upstairs bedroom."

Addie knew she had one chance, and one chance only, to prove to Ben and Emily that she wasn't a scaredy cat. She knew she was as brave as anyone and she wasn't about to let anyone or anything scare her now.

Creeping along the landing, she crept up to the bedroom door.

The moaning voice was just on the other side of the door, "I am the ghost of the bloody finger. I am in the upstairs bedroom." It sounded louder and scarier than ever before.

With trembling hands, Addie turned the door handle slowly, peering into the darkened room.

She couldn't see anything, but the voice seemed as if it was right next to her when it moaned quietly in her ear, "I am the ghost of the bloody finger. I am in the upstairs bedroom."

She turned and yelled, "Well, my name's Addie and you don't scare me. Quit your moaning and put a bandaid on it!"

The ghost was so surprised that it turned and ran. It ran back across the room with the cobwebs hanging from the chandelier, jumped through the window with paint peeling on the sash and ran down the creaky steps leading away from the front door. And it was never seen again, from that day to this.

And you probably won't be surprised to know that no-one ever dares to call Addie 'Shrimp'!

TWO

EVERY CLOUD HAS A SILVER LINING

It was Friday, the Thirteenth of June.

Lucy really didn't want to go to school that day and with good reason. Tomorrow, her Grandma was flying back to America.

That meant she wouldn't see her again until Christmas, when the whole family headed out west. All she wanted to do was spend one last day with her.

It was always so great when Grandma came to stay at Lucy's house, rather than the other way round.

Firstly, she always bought loads of presents with her. This year she had turned up with a giant Grizzly Bear.

'Why is it grizzly? Does that mean it's sad?' her little brother had asked. But then, he was much younger than her and not half as smart.

The bear was so big that Lucy was convinced Grandma must have bought it a separate seat on the plane.

'I did,' said Grandma, 'I even got a discount on his ticket because he didn't eat any of the in-flight meals.'

As lovely as Grandma was, sometimes she forgot her granddaughter was quite old now, so unlikely to be tricked by silly stories like that.

But she always forgave Grandma for her silly jokes. Mostly because she had also bought her a big box of Jolly Ranchers (Blue Raspberry flavour for Lucy, and Sour Apple for James), a rather lovely T shirt with a picture of the Mississippi River on it and cheese in a can, which Lucy loved, sprayed onto toast, topped with chopped tomatoes and ketchup.

'You look like you've got the weight of the world on your shoulders,' Grandma said that morning, as she got ready for school.

Lucy was feeling cross. As she ate her breakfast (the last spray of cheese on toasted French bread), she took a deep breath and realised that she would just have to get on with her day. She had a plan, she just had to stick to the plan.

'Many a muckle makes a mickle,' Grandma would say at times like this. But nobody had a clue what she was talking about.

Lucy had already tried the 'I've got a headache' ploy to get out of going to school, but Mom was too clever to fall for that.

'Then you'll be too poorly to come to the restaurant for dinner with us tonight,' Mom had said.

Although she didn't like to admit it, Mom had hit on the real reason for Lucy's 'headache'. She was sad to see Grandma go back home. And sadder still to miss out on today's trip to the theme park. It wasn't fair, her little brother was going and she was not.

'What time are we going to the park, Grandma?' James had looked hard at his sister while he said these words, guaranteed to wind her up.

He might only be five, and extremely annoying, but there was no denying that James was a clever kid. He knew exactly what to say or do to make her cross.

'Half past nine, the same time as I took Lucy at the weekend,' said Grandma, suddenly seeing what the problem was. 'But we'll only go if you are good, and stop being cheeky to your sister.'

Good old Gran. Lucy felt cheerful for the first time that morning. She stuck her tongue out at her irritating brother, then marched from the table to clean her teeth.

James' whining words – 'Muuuuuum, Lucy stuck her … ' were quickly lost in the noise of the running water.

Matters took a turn for the worse, but not straight away. She was in the playground before school had even started, and for a few moments it seemed like everything might go to plan.

'Roller coaster minus ten,' she had said to herself. Her watch told her it was ten minutes to nine, and her desperate scheme was nearing fruition.

It was clever, Lucy admitted to herself. No, in fact her plan was genius. Quite brilliant, if she said so herself.

It had come to her in the car when Mom had been rambling on about work. She always talked about work, and Lucy didn't always take any notice, but this morning when she went on about her 'nine o clock meeting' and 'not being late' and her 'big order from a new client,' an idea entered Lucy's head.

Mom had just said that it was a good job that Grandma was taking James out for the day, because now she didn't have to worry about him, blah, blah, rabbit, rabbit, when the thought hit her!

It had started with a moody whinge. 'What about me?' Lucy had thought. 'What if my headache comes back and I need collecting from school?'

Then she remembered that she didn't have a headache, and had just made that up so she could have a day off and go out with Gran.

Mom would never fall for her having a headache, but what if Mom didn't need to hear about it? (Don't tell me you've never pretended to be ill, just so you could stay home, not even just once?)

The idea which sprang into her mind was that if Mom was in a meeting, and Lucy was 'taken ill', then it would be Grandma who would have to rescue her.

The timing would be crucial. Lucy would need to be collected late enough so that Grandma wouldn't have time to collect her *and* take her home *and* ring Dad to come back from his work to look after her *and* still take James to the Theme Park - but not so late that she'd already set off on the journey.

That meant that nine 'o' clock was her deadline. It was early enough for the secretary to spend five minutes fussing, then to ring home just as Grandma was loading James into the baby seat (which she always called the booster seat he used, because it annoyed him. 'I'm not a baby!' he'd scream)

In order to collect Lucy and take James for his treat, Grandma would simply *have to* collect Lucy on the way to the theme park.

Yes, everything was slotting into place. Sometimes, Lucy had to admit, her genius surprised even her.

She could picture it now.

'I'll sit in the car,' she'd whimper, 'I'll be OK. Make sure (sniff) James enjoys his day. Don't worry about (dramatic pause) me.'

Acting like a martyr was guaranteed to get Grandma on her side. Who knows, if she opened the car window ('I'm desperate for fresh air') she might be able to get some pollen in her eyes and squeeze out a tear or two.

Then, just as the entrance to the park was reached, Lucy would make a remarkable recovery, and spend the day riding roller coasters and going on the ghost train and bashing James with her bumper car (that'd show him who was biggest and best!).

It was, she thought, a perfect plan. The only issue now was choosing what sickness or injury would be so bad that she'd need to be sent home.

Stomach pains and head aches were good because they didn't need visible symptoms. But, on the other hand, they could indicate something more serious and Grandma might decide that this risk outweighed her whining brother's demands to 'go on some rides.'

Actually, it would almost be worth the pleasure of seeing James' miserable face if Grandma did cancel the trip. But, 'don't cut off your nose to spite your face' was one of Gran's favourite sayings, and Lucy decided it definitely applied in this case. So what to do?

Then it came to her. She'd wait till Josie arrived, then they'd go and play in the corner where the school gardens were. None of the students in her class were very interested in gardening (they were mainly interested in football, fighting and fooling about, her class had poetically decided) these little plots were extremely overgrown with brambles and nettles.

Occasionally someone would fall in to them, and have to be seen by a teacher, bleeding and bumpy from prickles or stings.

Lucy realised it might be painful, for ten minutes at most, but short term pain delivered long term gain (another of Gran's sayings, usually about Lucy doing her homework or James eating his beans) and a day at the Theme Park was definitely a prize worth winning for the cost of ten minutes of discomfort.

Of course, she'd tell Josie of her plan – her friend would approve the scheme. Then she'd throw herself accidentally on purpose into the prickly shrubs, Josie would get help and Mrs Higginbottom, the school secretary, would hum and hah a little before deciding that Lucy needed to go home. Perfect.

Just then, Josie's Mom arrived at the gates with Josie's older sister Jemima and younger brother Jacob. But no Josie. 'Hello Mrs Williams, where's Josie?' asked Lucy, feeling rather worried that her plan seemed in danger of failing at the first hurdle.

Mrs Williams just shook her head.

'Day Diva[1],' said Jemima rather unclearly. Lucy was confused; everybody knew Josie could be a bit of a Princess when the mood took her, but a diva for a day? She wasn't into singing or opera or whatever, although she did do some ballet. Perhaps she'd thrown a tantrum over that?

'Der Day Diva's do dad dat dees daying din dead.' (*Her hay fever's so bad that she's staying in bed.*) Jemima really wasn't making much sense. At least, not until the last word.

'She's dead?' Lucy asked in shock.

'Do, din dead!' (*No, in bed*) replied Jemima. 'Dand dive dot dit as well, dut dum dade de dum do dool.' (*And I've got it as well, but Mom made me come to school*). And with that, Jemima gave her Mom one last grumpy look, and ran off to find her friends.

'No dear, don't worry,' said Mrs Johnstone. 'Josie's just got a bit of day diva, I mean hay fever. They all have', she pointed at the thick green snot pouring down like mouldy lava from Jacob's nose.

Josie's got her dance exam tomorrow, so I said she should rest up today. I'm afraid you'll have to play with someone else.'

And with that, Mrs Williams turned and left. Jacob wiped a hand across his upper lip, gave a long, bubbly sniff, licked his green fingers clean and ran off.

Drat! Plan A up the creek without a paddle, as Grandma might say.

But Lucy was not going to give up that easily. She could still make use of the nettles, and if she wailed loudly enough, surely somebody would go and get help. Normally, Lucy would have been enormously disappointed that Josie wasn't at school, but since she planned to soon be on her way out through the gates pretty soon, she wasn't all that bothered.

Then the next disaster of the day occurred. As she made her way across the playground, she could see the boiler suited back of Bill, the caretaker. He was standing right in the middle of the patch of nettles and brambles which she hoped would soon be her key to escape from school, and her ticket to the theme park.

'Don't mix your metaphors,' Grandma would have said, if she could read Lucy's mind. (To which Dad would quip 'My first girlfriend was the image of perfection but was as grumpy as a goat. In fact, I don't know what I met her for.' Lucy had no idea why he always laughed when he said it. Nobody else did.)

But metaphors were the last of her problems at the moment, because she realised her previous observation was not quite right. Old Bill was bending down in the brambles, but there were no brambles there! Nor any stinging nettles. Even the overgrown rose bush was gone. In fact, all that was left was a neatly dug patch of soil with just the odd bit of grass poking through.

'Don't come too close,' said the caretaker. 'I've put some weed killer down. Supposed to be harmless to pets and children, but you can never be too sure. I hope those gardening club maniacs appreciate it, took me four hours after school yesterday to clear these so-called 'gardens.'

At his words, Plan B took a kamikaze nose dive, right into the neatly dug school garden.

Lucy's bad day was getting worse. But she refused to give up.

'If at first you don't succeed, then try, try and try again.' Grandma would say.

Well, she might have reached the 'try again' stage, but she was certainly not beaten yet.

'Try every trick in the book,' that would be Gran's advice. Well, Lucy wasn't on the last page yet. In front of her lay a hard and bumpy playground. One full speed sprint accompanied by a spectacular fall would deliver the same results as a dive in a bush full of brambles.

'Lucy Stobart, can I borrow you please?'

'Oh no. No, no, no! Too late,' Miss Miller was calling her. It was Roller Coaster minus five, and that meant there was barely time to see what the teacher wanted, get back outside and do the deed.

'Yes, Miss.'

Lucy resigned herself to her fate. She trudged across to the smiling teacher who had an unwelcome message.

'I'm away on a course today,' she said 'and Mr Thacker is taking the class. Please could you help me set up the classroom for him?'

Not Mr Thacker! Thacker the Thwacker (as everyone called him when he was out of earshot) was the most hated teacher in the school. In fact, any school. A man so horrible they'd had to remove him from being a class teacher and turn him into a Headmaster.

Now she really had to escape. Suddenly, it was about more than going to the theme park with Gran; more than a last day out before Grandma flew back to the States; more even than avoiding a boring morning without Josie.

'Hope never dies,' Grandma would say, but hope was at death's door at the moment.

Lucy followed Miss Miller into their room and by the time she had laid out books, equipment and art materials, the bell had gone for registration. The rest of the class were in their seats and Mr Thacker the Thwacker was standing, hands on hips and looking even more red-faced and angry than usual, talking to Miss Miller.

Lucy glanced at her watch: it was Roller Coaster plus two. Time was up and her plan had failed.

She could hardly believe that her day could actually get worse. Lucy realised, sometimes it doesn't just rain, it pours, as Grandma was always saying. And then, you find you have forgotten your umbrella.

English was bad, Mr Thwacker grumpily explaining on the board how to use an apostrophe. Still, at least everybody could think about better things than apostrophes, since their teacher for the day spoke solidly for an hour. At the end, no-one was any wiser about where to put the apostrophe.

But while most of the class were just sitting there and thinking about the latest computer game or TV program, Lucy could not get a less pleasant thought out of her head. And that thought featured the image of a screaming, laughing James riding on the roller coaster.

Maths meant tedious tests about time; Lucy found the questions Mr Thwacker, sorry Thacker, was setting far too easy and found herself thinking up her own problems.

'If it takes a roller coaster three minutes to complete its circuit and the queue to get on is two minutes' long, how many times can James and Grandma ride the roller coaster in twenty minutes?[2]'

Or 'If candy floss takes three minutes to wind on its stick and ten minutes to eat how many can James consume in an hour?[3]'

Then, 'If a ride on the teacups lasts for five minutes, how many rides will James get before he vomits up all the ice cream Grandma has bought him?'

At least it was art after lunch, surely not even Mr Thacker could make that boring.

'Miss Miller wants you to paint a picture called *Where I would most like to be at the moment*. Personally,' went on the headmaster, 'I would prefer Miss Miller set you more grammar to do. I will have a word with her. I still have some tests to mark and haven't time to set you any proper work, so you'll just have to get on with it.'

Lucy had no problems choosing the subject of her picture, and was just adding some bright blue paint to her water flume when it happened.

The boys decided to make collages. All of them, at the same time!

Miss Miller never let more than two people make a collage at one time, because it always got out of control and a terrible mess ensued. But

Thwacker was too busy on his laptop, and kept his promise to 'let them get on with it.'

Silly man. Whilst he was engrossed in marking tests, mayhem broke out across the classroom. It was only when Mr Thacker finally looked up that he saw the state of the classroom.

There were pieces of paper, cut up cardboard, an unholy mess of material, glue and scissors. The floors and the tables were covered with tiny pieces paper and sticky glue. There were only five minutes to go till it was time for everyone to go home.

Fairness was not a word that came easily to Thacker the Thwacker's lips.

'This is a mess,' he shouted. 'Class, go and tell your parents that you'll be half an hour late today. Then will return here and clear up this mess!' he yelled.

The protests that it was the boys who had caused the chaos fell, as Grandma might say, on deaf ears. So the class slowly trooped out to tell their waiting parents that they had to stay behind to pick up all the litter on the classroom floor.

Lucy saw Grandma and James (looking rather green, she noted) and gave them the bad news.

'Sorry Grandma,' she said. 'It's going to be another half an hour before we can go home. We have to pick up all the mess and litter the boys made in the classroom. I don't know where to begin!'

But Grandma even had an answer to this.

'Don't know how to collect litter?' she said. 'No problem, just make a start and you'll pick it up as you go along.'

Lucy trudged back to the classroom, fed up at how the day had turned out. As she walked in to the classroom, Billy asked her a question. It was as she turned to answer him, that it happened.

Just at that moment she was standing in a particularly wet and gloopy patch of glue. As she twisted round to answer Billy, her feet went one way and her body went the other. She found herself gliding down to the floor and, with a crash, her arm hit the desk on the way down.

When she came to, something seemed to be wrong with her hand. It seemed to be at the wrong angle to her arm, she was pretty sure it didn't normally look like that.

Sure enough, Mrs Higginbottom was called for and duly pronounced that Lucy had 'probably broken something.'

An ambulance was called and, accompanied by Grandma and James, they had a thrilling ride to the hospital. Lucy hadn't been in an ambulance before and she was quite sure this was just as exciting as some of the rides that James had been on earlier that day.

Soon Lucy, Grandma and James emerged from the hospital, with Lucy's wrist encased in bright purple plaster.

'Come on love, let's get you home,' said Grandma, as they hopped into a waiting taxi.

Back home, Grandma made sure Lucy was seated comfortably, propped up by plenty of soft cushions. Then she suggested that Lucy put on her favourite movie, 'to help her recuperate'. Poor James didn't get a look in.

'I've just spoken with your Mom. I've changed my flight and I'm going to stay on for another week. The doctor said you should stay out of school for a couple of days, so I thought I'd stay to help Mom out.'

"That's great Grandma!"

'Would you like some Vanilla Toffee Fudge ice cream with toffee sauce?' asked Grandma.

'Yes please Grandma,' Lucy replied.

'By the way, I've ordered some pizza to be delivered, it won't be long in coming,' said Grandma.

James groaned quietly and sat playing computer games in the corner.

Lucy smiled and thought to herself, 'you know, Grandma is right about one thing, 'every cloud really does have a silver lining."

---

1. Hayfever
2. The answer is four times.
3. The answer is 4 (or 4 and a half, if you're being pernickety, as Grandma might say).

THREE

THE FIRST FIRE (A CHEROKEE MYTH)

When the world was created, there was no fire and the world was cold.

Only the Thunder Gods had fire. One day the Thunder Gods sent a bolt of lightning to earth. The lightning struck the bottom of a hollow sycamore tree, growing in the middle of an island.

Each of the animals watched, as a plume of smoke rose from the base of the tree on the island. And smoke meant fire!

The animals were desperate to bring fire and it's warmth into their world, but could not reach it, because of the water surrounding the island.

As was their tradition, they held a council of all the animals, to decide how to get the fire.

Raven was first to speak, asking if he might fly across to the island. Raven was big, strong and white. The animals all agreed that he could bring back fire.

So Raven flew high into the sky, and landed on the sycamore tree. But the fire scorched his feathers black and he flew back, without fire. That is why the Raven's feathers are black to this day.

Next, Screech Owl asked if he could go. He flew across to the tree and perched on a branch. As he looked down towards the flames, the hot air from the fire rose and burnt his eyes. He made his way home, but his eyes were sore for many days. That is why the Screech Owl's eyes are red to this day.

Then Hooting Owl and Horned Owl asked to go, but the rising smoke made rings around their eyes. That is why the Hooting and Horned Owl's have white rings around their eyes, to this day.

A little black snake said he would go through the water and bring back fire. He swam through the deep water, crawled through the long grass until at last he reached the sycamore tree. He slithered inside the tree, through a hole at its base.

But the fire had left hot ashes at the base of the tree, and it was too hot for the little black snake who raced quickly out of the tree, darting this way and that, trying to cool down.

Ever since that day, the little black snake darts this way and that, trying to escape from the hot ashes.

There was still no fire and the world remained cold.

By now, all of the animals, birds and snakes were afraid to cross to the island to bring back fire.

All except one.

The water spider said that she would go.

"How will you bring back the fire?" asked the other animals.

"Watch and learn," said the water spider, and with that, she spun a bowl, which she placed on her back. Off she ran, across the top of the water, until she reached the island.

She ran through the grass to the base of the sycamore tree. Carefully, she placed one small, burning ember into her bowl and, running back across the top of the water, returned to the waiting animals.

That is why the water spider still has the bowl on her back and that is how the world got fire, and because of the brave water spider, we have had fire here ever since.

FOUR

THE PURPLE GORILLA

"Come on Logan!" called Scout.

"Alright, I'm coming," replied Logan.

Logan parked the pickup truck, leaving the keys in the ignition.

This far into the woods, no-one would even see the truck, let alone think of stealing it.

The truck door closed with a satisfying "CLUNK".

This was it, their first weekend camping together. They'd been planning it for weeks and now it was here, their excitement level was high.

They'd been dreaming of nights in the woods, sleeping in hammocks which swung gently in the wind, as they looked up through the tree tops to the starry sky above.

The weather was perfect - the sky was clear and the stars were just starting to come out. Without the pollution of the city lights, they could make out the star constellations in the sky above their heads.

"Look, Orion's belt!" exclaimed Scout.

"First things first," said Logan. "Let's get a fire lit."

Scout, who'd been a Cub Scout for several years, and then had been a fully fledged Scout, was eager to demonstrate some fire-making skills.

Within minutes, there was a roaring fire, its bright flames crackling and lighting up the dark forest.

Scout set up the stick to cook the bacon over the open fire, just like they'd been shown at Scouts. The bacon hung over the stick, above the fire, and was soon sizzling wildly, the bacon fat dripping down into the flames below.

Soon Logan and Scout sat munching the delicious bacon sandwiches in silence and looking up at the stars.

When they finished eating, Logan began to tell a favorite campfire story.

"Quit pushing me around," shouted Addie at her big brother, Ben ...

And Logan went on to tell the scariest story that Scout had ever heard, about a ghost and a bloody finger.

When the story ended they both fell silent, listening to the eerie sounds of the forest around them.

"HOOOO...!" The sound of an owl calling out in the dark sent shivers down their spin. It was awesome to hear.

"ARF ARF," the sound of dogs barking in the distance was reassuring - they weren't so far from home as it felt at this moment.

"Those animals sound scary," said Scout.

"That's nothing, you should hear the sound of the animal my Dad keeps hidden away," said Logan, almost immediately regretting speaking.

"What do you mean?" asked Scout.

"Oh, nothing," said Logan quietly.

"You have to tell now, you can't start something and not finish it."

"Well, I've only seen it once. I snuck in behind Dad, when he wasn't watching. You won't believe me if I tell you anyway."

"Try me," said Scout.

"OK. Our property comes with several acres. One day when I was following Dad I discovered it."

"Discovered what?" asked Scout.

"An old underground shelter. It's huge! They built it back in the 60's when they thought we'd all get destroyed by a nuclear bomb. It was decommissioned but it's still on our land."

"What's that to do with the scary animal your Dad keeps hidden away?"

"That's where he keeps it, in the old shelter."

"You're just trying to scare me," said Scout, "it sounds like something out of a sci-fi movie. That kind of thing doesn't happen in real life."

"It does and I'll prove it to you," replied Logan.

"Go on then, I dare you!" said Scout.

"OK then. We'll go in the morning, but you have to promise not to tell anyone. It'll be our secret."

"Agreed," said Scout.

And so it was, that Scout and Logan burrowed down to sleep in their hammocks, dreaming of scary monsters hidden in deep underground shelters.

They woke at dawn, grabbed their camping gear and threw it into the back of the truck.

Soon they were on their way to Logan's home, parking up a block away, so as not to wake Logan's parents.

"CREAK," they pushed their way through a crack in the wooden fence.

Walking through tall pine trees, their footsteps noiseless on the soft pine needled floor.

"Not far now," Logan whispered.

Now they were making their way through broken twigs and branches on the forest floor. "CRUNCH, CRUNCH, CRUNCH!"

They came upon a clearing, with an enormous outcrop of rock, into which was fixed a wide metal doorway. Above the doorway hung a battered old sign, saying *"Danger, keep out."*

Scout gasped, rather surprised to realise that this wasn't just another of Logan's elaborate pranks.

A flutter of nervousness flitted through Scout's stomach.

"What is the animal that Logan's Dad keeps hidden", wondered Scout, "and why?"

Logan reached into a back pocket and pulled out a key. Turning the key in the lock, "CLANG," the heavy metal door opened slowly, to reveal a dark interior.

"There's a light switch somewhere. The old wiring and lighting are all still in place," said Logan. Reaching for a switch, the light illuminated a huge stairway, leading down into the blackness beyond.

Above the stairway a sign said, *"Danger. Do not go beyond this point."*

"Come on, I can't wait to show you," said Logan.

"CLUNK, CLUNK, CLUNK," went their footsteps, as they descended the metal stairs.

"BANG!". In the dark, Scout walked right into one of the tables.

Another light switch revealed a wide open space, with lots of old equipment on creaky old tables, just gathering dust.

Leading off to the left, was a long tunnel.

Hanging from the tunnel roof was a large sign saying *"Turn back."*

"This way," said Logan.

Scout followed behind along the tunnel, until they came to a strange glass door. Logan pressed a red button and 'SWOOSH', the door slid open and they passed through.

Cobwebs hung from the tunnel ceiling.

"This feels creepy," thought Scout.

"Not far now," said Logan.

Leading the way, they passed through a series of doorways.

"CLICK" went the first door.

"SQUEAK" went the second door, which needed a good oiling of its hinges.

"GROAN" went the third door, as it swung on heavy hinges.

"THUD" went the next door, as it closed behind them to reveal a single door in front of them.

"It's behind that door," said Logan. "You must be completely quiet. Don't say a word, don't even breathe. And whatever you do, don't touch what you see behind that door."

Scout was beginning to wish they'd just stayed in the truck, but it was too late to say anything now.

Besides, Scout was curious, what kind of animal was locked up behind the door and why?

The sign on the door in front of them was in big letters and read *"No Entry, this means YOU!"*

The final door swung open, and shut behind them. "CHING!"

Scout stared in amazement. In the very centre of the room was an enormous cage and inside that enormous cage, lay an enormous purple gorilla, fast asleep and snoring loudly.

"Amazing!" whispered Scout, just loudly enough for Logan to hear. Logan nodded in agreement.

For a while they both stood staring at the creature in front of them.

"We'd better get out of here," said Logan, "my Dad'll be coming back soon."

Logan turned to go and unlocked the door, "CHING!"

Scout turned to take one final look at the gorilla and reached out a hand, curious to touch the gorilla's purple hair.

"RRRAAAAARRR!!" the gorilla roared, it was now wide awake. It stood up in its cage and towered over Scout. "RRRAAAAAR!" it roared again, rattling the bars of the cage.

Suddenly those cage bars didn't look so strong now.

Without looking back, Logan and Scout began to run.

They ran through the doors, "THUD' went the first door behind them. "GROAN" creaked the second door. "SQUEAK" went the next door, and "CLICK' went the final door.

Above the final door was a sign which read *I warned you.*

Behind them they could hear the "RRRAAR!" of the gorilla, as it followed closely behind them.

They came to the glass door and pressed the red button, "SWOOSH" the door opened, as they ran through the tunnel.

Above their heads, a sign read *I told you so.*

"BANG" they both ran right into the dusty old tables, before running "CLUNK, CLUNK, CLUNK," up the metal stairway, opening the entrance door "CLANG" and running 'CRUNCH, CRUNCH, CRUNCH," across the forest floor.

"CREAK" went the wooden fence, as they slid through the broken panel.

Scout reached the truck, hands shaking.

Jumping in, Scout turned the key in the ignition and the engine jumped into life.

Too late. Scout and Scout turned, there was the gorilla, so close they could feel his breath.

Helpless, Scout and Logan sat, frozen to the spot, as the gorilla effortlessly tore off the truck door.

They both closed their eyes and waited for the inevitable. They'd ignored the warnings, they deserved what happened next.

They heard the awful sound of the gorilla roaring and beating its breast. Then, an enormous finger reached out and touched Scout on the shoulder.

"TAG, you're it!"

FIVE

LOST IN YELLOWSTONE - THE TRUE STORY OF TRUMAN EVERTS

My name is Truman Everts. Before we get started, I must warn you that Lost in Yellowstone is a true story. It happened to me, just as I am about to tell it to you.

I'd heard stories about the beauty of the Rocky Mountains while living in Montana. I'd listened to strange tales of the Yellowstone.

I began to imagine that participating in an Expedition to Yellowstone would be both interesting and worthwhile.

I supposed that the hardships of traveling by horseback through the rough terrain would be well rewarded by the grandeur of the natural scenery, of which I'd heard tell.

Of course, the thought of getting utterly lost, without food; the concept of wandering for days in the wilderness, was something I had not once considered.

Some days into our expedition, I became separated from my companions. Our way was blocked by a dense pine forest, fallen trees, which made progress almost impossible.

As I tried to make my way past one of these enormous trees laying prostrate on the forest floor, I happened to stray out of sight and hearing of my companions.

It had been a busy day, and it was late in the afternoon. I was tired, and perhaps it was for this reason that becoming separated from my friends didn't give me any cause to worry. I rode onwards, confident that I'd soon be rejoining my friends and sharing the story around the campfire.

I rode on until darkness made traveling through the dense forest too dangerous. To have no sustenance for the evening was indeed disagreeable, but I smiled to myself as I imagined telling the story to my friends around the campfire.

On the following day, I rose at dawn, mounted my horse and rode in what I felt sure was the direction of our camp. I could picture my friends camping on the lake shore, awaiting my arrival.

The falling pine needles had obliterated any trace of the trail for which I was searching. The best I could do was to examine the ground in vain for tracks or indications that my companions had traveled this way.

I came to a clearing in the forest where there were several ways forward. I dismounted my horse, intending to choose which track which would lead me in the direction of my companions. I took a few paces into the forest.

As I was searching the ground for tracks, my horse took fright, and I turned around, to see him disappearing at full tilt through the forest. That was the last time I saw him.

Everything, except the clothing I stood up in, my opera glasses and a couple of knives, had been attached to the horse's saddle - my blankets, gun, matches and fishing tackle had all vanished with my horse.

Even so, I was not anxious. The thought that I could be permanently separated from my companions was not something which I had entertained. Instead, I spent my efforts on trying to track down the horse, albeit in vain.

Realizing that I was indeed separated from my companions, I wrote some notes for them and posted them along my route, in case they should pass this way.

After this, I struck out into the forest, heading in the direction of their camp. As the day passed, I began to feel alarmed at the thought of spending another night alone, without either food or fire.

Yet, I continued to hope that I would soon come across my friends and we would all soon be laughing at my strange adventure.

As I pressed on, I began to realize that I could be in real danger. I sat down on a log, trying to figure out my next step.

As best as I could guess, my companions must have passed close to the spot where I had placed the notices and would now be waiting for me to rejoin them. As darkness was falling, I realised that I must spend yet another night alone, before rejoining them.

I spent the night on a bed of pine needles, in the pitch dark, now more aware than ever of the danger I was in. As I looked upwards through the tree branches, the wind sighed through the pine, and the forest was alive with the barking of coyotes and the long howl of the gray wolf. These same sounds had accompanied us many nights on our travel thus far, but tonight they filled me with terror. Sleep came fitfully.

I awoke and pushed forward to the place where I had posted my notice. No-one had passed this way. I sat down, overwhelmed with disappointment. For the first time, the realization came over me that I was lost.

Not only lost, but lost without food or means to make a fire. I was alone in the wilderness, over a hundred miles from human habitation and surrounded by wild animals.

To stop myself from becoming despondent, I resolved in my mind, "not to perish in the wilderness."

I still hoped that I would be able to rejoin my party, if I could only find the location of their camp.

I rose from my seat and pushed my way through the thick forest branches. A feeling of physical weakness replaced hunger.

From time to time, as I scrambled over a fallen tree or pushed through a thicket, a sense of exhaustion would come over me. Each time I felt like sinking, I'd say out loud, "I simply must find my friends."

In my worst imaginings, I'd think of my daughter, and how news of my starvation or terrible death might reach her.

At this time, a recent debate was brought to mind, in which we had discussed whether each man had within him the self-preservation skills necessary to rise to any emergency. This spurred me on, as I felt that it must indeed be so.

I now record this thought, so that anyone who might read this, if you ever find yourself in a similar situation, may not succumb to despair, however desperate it might at first seem. Such a thought can give life to hope, stem hunger and revive the spirit.

It was noon when I stepped out of the forest into an open space. My surroundings were undeniably magnificent, with the lake before me glittering in the sunlight.

As I approached the sand at the lakeshore, I observed that rising above me was the loftiest peak of mountains, that appeared never-ending. The sparkling jet of a geyser, with the rising mists from the many hot springs, made this one of the most impressive landscapes I had ever seen.

Never before had I seen so much wildlife - mink and beaver swam around me unafraid; deer and elk looked at me in a surprised fashion and otters swam in and out of the water with astounding agility.

In any other circumstances, this scene would have transfixed me with amazement; yet, tired, anxious and hungry, I struggled to take it all in or even appreciate the fact that I was probably the first man to behold this incredible sight. Instead, I longed only for the comfort of friends, food and a shelter over my head.

On the second day by the lake, while gazing out at the vast expanse of water, I spotted a canoe, with a single oarsman at the helm.

It was moving towards me fast. I rose and hastened to the beach, encouraged that, whoever it was, I would soon have food and be restored to my friends.

As I drew closer, it turned northwards, and the object of my hope turned out to be a large pelican, which flapped its wings and flew further up the shore.

This small incident completely demoralized me. In one moment, my joy turned to significant loss and a new awareness of the horror of my situation.

Even so, I knew darkness was approaching, so I began to look for a spot to rest for the night. As I did so, I found a small thistle-like plant, which seemed strange amongst the pines. Pulling it up by the root, it looked somewhat like a radish. I bit into it; it was palatable and nourishing. And so, I feasted on thistle root, it was my first meal in four days.

Eureka! At last, I had found food. With food, I realized that I could manage until I was able to find my friends once again. What a contrast to the misery of the past hour, and the disappearing canoe!

With hunger held at bay, I lay down beneath a tree, its many branches stretching out above me and fell asleep.

I have no idea how long I slept for, but I was woken suddenly by a loud scream, something like a human being in pain.

I knew that sound. I had heard it many times. It was the screech of a mountain lion, and it was alarmingly nearby.

For a moment every nerve in my body froze in terror. Then my instincts kicked in and I was rapidly ascending the branches of the tree, shouting back down towards the ground. I quickly rose among the branches until I was as high as I could safely climb.

Below me, I could hear the animal snuffling and prowling, on the exact spot on which I had been sleeping just moments before.

Each time the mountain lion roared, I would respond with a loud scream.

To try and alarm the lion, I broke off branches, hurling them down towards it. The lion continued circling the tree, roaring and lashing the ground with his tail.

My attempts to frighten it off had failed. I resigned myself to my fate. At that moment, I realized that I had not tried silence. Holding fast to the tree trunk, I stayed perfectly still.

Below me, the snuffling and prowling continued, though the silence was ever more terrible, as I waited for the lion to pounce.

Minutes passed like hours. I have no concept how long the lion prowled beneath me. At last, with a bound, it ran off into the forest. I was alive!

If I'd had the strength, I would have stayed aloft the tree until morning, but my ordeal had left me much weakened and I descended its limbs slowly. I lay down on the forest floor, where only recently the beast had been prowling and fell into a deep sleep.

When I awoke, all that had happened the night before seemed like a terrible nightmare, only the broken branches around me were testament to the reality of my experience.

Once again my thoughts turned to home, and my loved ones who might never have known my terrible fate, had I perished that night.

As I pondered this, an easterly wind brought a storm of snow, mixed with rain (the sort that happens at high altitudes) which set in. My clothing, torn as it was from the undergrowth, left me exposed to the elements.

I knew from experience that this storm would not blow over quickly. The hope of finding my friends now gone, I knew with certainty that if I were to escape this wilderness, it would have to be from my own efforts.

I realized that my situation was grave and that I must act, and quickly. Spreading the branches of a spruce tree over me, pulling over earth and branches for warmth. I lay there for two days, while the storm raged about me.

Only one thing transpired during those dismal days - a cold bird, hopped within arm's reach - starved and hungry, I grabbed it and killed it, devouring it raw.

On the third day, the storm abated and I made my path towards the hot springs in the shadow of the mountain.

I was chilled to the bone, my clothing wet through. I lay down next to a tree, the ground warm beneath me from the hot springs. Once the warmth started to permeate my body, I staved my hunger with a snack of thistle-roots.

Nearby I built a shelter of pine branches and hid here until the storm blew over. Thistles were plentiful here, and I felt they could sustain me, for the moment.

I stayed here for seven days, the first three of which the storm continued to rage and blow around me. Meanwhile, the vapor from the hot springs enveloped me, as if I was in a warm bath.

Hidden away here, all I could do was eat, sleep and think. My thoughts were given over to how best I could escape from this wilderness.

The want of fire was what most concerned me. I recalled everything I'd read about the making of fire, but to no avail. I knew that without the ability to make fire, escape from the wilderness was impossible. I'd either be attacked by wild beasts or perish in another storm, like the one which had just passed. It was only the warmth of the hot springs which had saved me on this occasion.

A thick layer of snow had fallen, and I hid in my pine branch refuge until it disappeared. As I lay there, I dreamt of creating some memorial, so that one day a passerby might know what became of me.

A ray of sunlight lit up the lake with sparkles, and with it, an idea came to my mind. There was a lens in my opera glasses, by which I could procure fire.

I immediately fell upon the task - imagine my joy when I saw the beauty of smoke curling from the dry wood I held between my fingers.

At that moment I felt that, if the whole world were offered in exchange, I would deny it all, before parting with that precious spark.

I now had both food and fire, though the food was barely sufficient, yet with a fire now kindled, my hunger was momentarily forgotten.

In an unhappy accident, I managed to scald my hip which, added to my frostbitten feet, made movement harder and caused delays.

I had mislaid both my knives, so I managed to fashion a replacement by sharpening a buckle. With this, I managed to fashion some footwear, held together by strips of bark. Unraveling my handkerchief, I was able to mend my clothes. From the same material, I formed a fishing line, which attached to a pin, fashioned as a fish-hook.

On the morning of the eighth day of my arrival at the hot springs, I ventured forth on the next step of my journey.

The morning was beautiful, the sun was warm, and the air was fresh. For a moment, I felt exhilaration, that is until I felt once more my utter aloneness and separation from my companions.

From this day on, the days without food began to take a toll on me. It felt as if my mind was in a dreamland and I had strange imaginings.

The wind changed, and the sky clouded over, bringing colder air and the need for a warm fire. I pulled out my glass lens, but alas, there was no sun to shine. I sat down, waiting for a shaft of sunlight to break through, but night came, and the freezing cold found me on a bleak hillside, half-starved and barely clothed.

I believe that I only survived the long and terrible night by pacing up and down, rubbing my numb hands and feet against a log. Frozen, I retraced my steps to the lakeside, building my first fire by the beach and recovering there for a further two days.

If there had been the slimmest hope that my friends might search for me and find me, this now left me altogether. I knew that it was by my own exertions that I would have to escape.

I sat to plan my escape from the wilderness. I had a choice of three routes. One was to follow Snake River for about a hundred miles; another to cross the country by scaling the Madison Mountains; and the other, was to retrace my journey by which I had come to this place.

The last of these was the least inviting, as I was so familiar with the difficulties I would face.

I'd heard that the waters of the Snake River were hazardous, so dared not choose that route.

This left me with one choice, to travel across the Madison range, which seemed the shortest, yet proved to be a most unwise decision, as you shall see shortly.

I filled my pockets with thistle-roots and started for Yellowstone Lake. I stopped at noon to make fire, while the sun was highest in the sky and kept a small brand burning through regular blowing.

That night I lit a fire amid a dense thicket of pines. Around me, I could hear the screaming of night-birds, the Mountain lion and the wolves howling.

I sat with my back against a tree, the smoke from the fire enveloping me.

As I half sat, half lay there, I imagined blazing eyes in the thick forest; I fancied a pack of wolves ready to pounce on me in the darkness. I slept fitfully, longing for morning to come.

At dawn, I resumed my journey towards the lake. Sunset found me at a headland with a magnificent view of the mountains and valley - the peaks of the three Tetons rose in the distance. To my right, the Madison mountains with their ravines, canons, and gorges glittered in the sunlight.

As I looked out at the magnificent panorama before me, I nearly forgot to make the most of the rays of the sun, to get a small firebrand burning.

Holding the brand in my hand, I descended to the beach of the lake. I kindled a fire and, kicking off my hand-fashioned shoes, walked barefoot along the soft, warm sand, gathering wood for the fire.

As dusk fell, I looked around for my slippers. One was found, but the other was missing. There was no option but to search for it, combing the hill-side and beach. After an hour my search was rewarded with the joyous discovery of the missing slipper.

Finally, I was able to rest - sitting on the sand and listening to the wild lullaby of the roaring waves.

After a refreshing sleep, I woke, stirred the remaining embers into flame and ate a cheery breakfast.

I resumed my journey, walking along the lakeshore - finding at noon, the camp where my friends stayed.

I found a dinner fork, which I pressed into service for digging roots and a yeast-powder can, which became my drinking cup. Though I look around for food, I found none (though I later discovered that they had indeed hidden some closer to where I had initially strayed from the camp). Dejected by this disappointment, I retraced my steps along the beach.

A spot of sunshine in the afternoon, allowed me to light a firebrand, which I carried to my camping place to build a fire. The wind had picked up, so making a shelter of pine branches, I crawled under it and was soon asleep.

I have no idea how long I slept there - but the sound of snapping, crackling and hissing woke me.

Both my shelter of branches and the nearby forest were on fire. My left hand was severely burned, and the fire had singed my hair back, as I escaped this ring of fire. In my hasty escape, I lost my buckle-tongue knife, my pin fish-hook, and tape fishing line.

The pine forest was soon a vast sheet of flame, the flames shooting hundreds of feet into the night sky, lighting up the lake and mountains around me. It was both terrible and full of grandeur. The sound of burning and falling branches was deafening, the air filled with acrid smoke. On and on it burned, until it felt as if the entire hillside was afire.

When the fire passed, all that remained was a blackened trail of devastation.

I could no longer search for a trail, so resolved to aim for the lowest part of the Madison range. For many hours, I made my way over the rugged hills, through fallen trees and thorny thickets.

The mountains mocked me, receding into the distance as I advanced.

I had taken the precaution of obtaining fire, so slept in warmth that night. The idea of finding a hidden pass into the Madison filled me with hope.

As I came closer, all I could see were endless peaks and precipices, rising thousands of feet sheer above the plain. There was no hidden gully or pass to help me through. Despair overwhelmed me. The last two days had been wasted; it was all in vain.

My only option now seemed to be down the Yellowstone. I felt strong enough to spend one more day searching for a pass. I had presumed that the thistles would be growing everywhere, so my supply was already gone. I searched the hillside in vain for them.

I needed to decide whether to search for a way through the Montana range or return to the Yellowstone.

It was at this time that I experienced the most strange hallucination. An old friend, whose wisdom I had always valued, appeared before me.

"Go back immediately, as rapidly as your strength permits. There is no food here, and the idea of scaling these rocks is madness."

"Doctor," I replied. "It's too far; I cannot make it."

"Your life depends on it. Return at once my friend; it is your only chance," he urged. "Travel as fast as you can."

But Doctor," I replied, "My companions are just a few miles away. My strength is almost gone, my shoes are worn out, and my clothes are in tatters. I will climb this mountain or die trying."

"Don't even think of it. I will accompany you. Help yourself, and God will help you."

Persuaded at last and thrilled to have the Doctor as my traveling companion, I returned whence I had come.

After walking a few miles, I kindled a fire and slept peacefully.

As I started out the following morning, the sun was rising. From time to time, I would question the wisdom of taking this route, and as I did so, my old friend the Doctor would appear to offer some words of encouragement.

In the high altitudes of the mountains, distance is deceptive. After walking for two days, my destination seemed as far away as it had when I had set out.

On the afternoon of the fourth day, I kindled a fire and gathered some roots - they were the first thing I'd eaten in five days. As I lay down that night, I felt that my hopes of escape were slipping from my grasp.

At dawn, I started down the trail. My motto, "I will not perish in this wilderness," often came to mind and revived my spirits a little.

As I struggled through a mass of tangled trees which seemed never-ending, I paused to seriously consider whether it might be better to stop and die quietly here, than to pursue my plan of escape. The idea of escape seemed only to prolong my suffering.

A voice seemed to whisper to me across the wind, "While there is life, there is hope. Take courage." My thoughts thus disrupted, I rose and carried on.

I came to a clearing and found the fresh tip of a gull's wing. At once I kindled a fire, ground the wing to a powder, and made a broth of sorts, which I consumed with relish. At once I fell into a deep sleep.

I had reached the point where I no longer felt hungry; such was my starvation. Indeed, time itself seemed to be unimportant. Days and nights came and went. My mind wandered.

As I slept my dreams took me to fabulous restaurants in New York and Washington. I would sit down to enormous feasts and delicious dainties, and I imagined myself eating these delights until I was replete. Alas! The feasts were only in my dreams.

I arrived at the falls on a cold day, when the wind was moaning through the pines. The scene which had so captivated me only weeks before held no interest for me.

I waited in vain for a single ray of sunshine, with which to kindle a fire. But the sun remained hidden. There would be no fire that night.

I set about building a shelter of brushwood, with fallen leaves as my bed. Though I tried to sleep, the cold permeated my body, and it was only by rubbing my hands together and beating my legs that I did not freeze in my shelter that night.

When I rose the next morning, I was practically paralyzed with cold. I managed to make my way to the river and sat waiting for the sun to make its appearance.

Nothing in the majestic surroundings compared to the beauty of the sun coming out from behind the clouds and shining down on my glass lens. I kindled a flame, which I fed with every stick and branch I could gather and sat by it, warming myself through for several hours.

Just a short distance away the Yellowstone falls roared, but they had lost all their charm for me.

The Doctor who had been present with me until this point, now left me and was not seen again.

One day, I came across a stream, filled with small fish. I plunged my hands into the water, grabbed a handful and devoured them raw. This was a feast!

My stomach disagreed, and I found myself very sick indeed. I was thankful that I had not eaten more, as had been my desire. If I had done so, there's little doubt that I would have died, alone in the wilderness, in excruciating torment.

My mind wandered to the dark waters of despair, and I would long for the release of death. Then I would recall all that had happened on my journey - the incident with the mountain lion, the blazing forest fire and my return from the Madison ranges, at the request of the doctor. In all of these, I could sense mysterious protection. Where was my mysterious protector now, when I needed a little faith to take me onwards?

I thought of my daughter and longed to be restored to her, even if only for an hour.

Along the streams, I would often sit and try to catch a trout, using a hook that I had fashioned from my broken spectacles. I never had success.

If only I had my gun, there was game aplenty around me - I saw herds of antelope, elk, deer; I saw flocks of geese, ducks, and pelicans; even the occasional bear. I had no way to kill them, so I found their presence irksome.

One afternoon, I came upon a large hollow tree, near "Tower Falls." The many tracks around it gave me to believe that it was a bear's den. The inside looked most inviting as a place to rest.

Accordingly, I gathered wood and twigs, lit a circle of fires around the tree and climbed into the hollow tree for the night. When I awoke, I saw that the flames had burnt a large area of the nearby forest, which had doubtless saved me from the rightful owner of the den and any further adventures.

Arriving at "Tower Falls" I once again tried in vain to hook myself a trout. I tried to capture a grasshopper and finally determined that I would eat only thistles from this point onwards.

I left "Tower Falls" and entered the open country. The forest gave way to a desolate landscape, with only the occasional clump of dwarf trees.

I made camp that night and woke to find wind and snowstorm had nearly extinguished my fire. With everything white with snow, I entirely lost my bearings. My only option was to find the river again and follow the direction of it's current.

Once I came to the edge of the canyon, below which lay the river, with great difficulty, I made my way down its rocky face. I drank with gusto from the pure waters and sat there for a while, hoping that the storm would soon pass, so that I could kindle a fire.

As the hours passed, it became clear that the sun would not be blessing me with an appearance. Chilled to the bone and soaked through, I scrambled up the canyon walls. It was hard work, and it was dark by the time I returned to my fire, which had nearly been blown out by the raging storm.

I lay two nights beside the fire, while the storm blew around me. Every night I would gather wood, brush and broken branches. I would snatch sleep in between these endeavours, and so I got little rest.

By this time, my arms had shrunk and were so thin that a small child could easily have put their hand right around them. "Yet," I told myself, "It is death to remain. I cannot perish in this wilderness."

As the sun rose, the snow rapidly melted and I continued my journey. Before leaving the forest, I had filled my pockets with thistles, knowing I was unlikely to find them in the open country beyond. As such, I had to ration myself, according to the number of days it would take me to reach civilization.

Two or three days before I was found, while climbing a steep slope, I collapsed from exhaustion into a bush. Without the energy to get up, I unbuckled my belt and fell asleep there.

When I woke, I fastened my belt and rose, continuing my course. Alas! When night fell, I gathered some brush for a fire and felt for my lens to kindle a flame. It was gone. If the earth had opened up to swallow me alive, I could not have been more alarmed. Without it, I was a dead man.

I lay down, overwhelmed with torment at my situation. My battle to escape the wilderness was over. As I lay there, the events of my life came before me, as in a dream.

After a while, my terror left me, and I came to myself. Thinking back I realized that I must have mislaid my glass when I had fallen asleep in the bush. There was only one course of action; I must retrace my steps to retrieve it. Imagine the joy and relief with which I found my lens in that exact spot.

Returning to my camp, I lit the brushwood, and lay down to rest. It began to snow, to keep the fire alive became principal purpose. I got no sleep that night.

The storm was still raging when I awoke, but I knew I must go on, in spite of it. Picking up a brand from the fire, I recommenced my journey.

After midday, the storm died down, and the sun made an appearance. Finding a small group of trees, I went about making my camp for the night; collecting wood and brush, together with some dry twigs, setting the brand down while I did so. In those short minutes, the brand expired, and though I blew on it to revive it, it was too late. It was late in the afternoon, and the sun was behind the clouds, I feared another freezing night without fire.

I sat there, holding my lens, waiting to catch a ray of sunlight. It felt as if my very life depended on it.

After a few moments, the clouds moved on, and the sun shone down.

With trembling hands I held my lens as steadily as I could, anxious in case another cloud should obscure the sunlight. My patience was rewarded with a small plume of smoke, making its way heavenwards. Shortly after, the spark became a flame which warmed me all through that night.

In the morning, I continued my way onwards. By now, I was sure I should no longer rely on the sun for warmth, but carry a brand with me, or die.

I walked for a fair distance, but then the storm came on, and I was chilled to the bone. I tried to kindle a fire, but could not make it burn well. Picking up a brand, I stumbled on, convinced that the end was near. I had done everything humanly possible to escape the wilderness, but I knew that I was days away from death.

As I was now on the trail, there was some small relief in knowing that my remains would one day be found and the mystery of my fate ended.

Even then, I heard a small voice seem to whisper, "struggle on."

As I groped along the hillside, I became aware of a reflection. Looking upwards, two faces met my gaze.

"Are you Mr. Everts?"

"Yes. All that is left of him."

"We have come for you."

"Who sent you?"

"Judge Lawrence and other friends."

"God bless him and them and you! I am saved!" And with these words, after 37 days in the wilderness, I fell into their arms falling into a state of unconsciousness.

Baronet and Prichette made camp at that very spot. One left to get help from Fort Ellis, some seventy miles hence, the other waited with me, and took care of me.

Within two days, I was strong enough to be moved some miles down the trail to a miner's cabin.

I rested in a proper bed, a game broth was made, and the miners abandoned their work to help restore me to health.

The night after I arrived at the cabin I was suffering the deepest agonies. I feared that I had been saved from the wilderness, only to die amongst friends.

As I lay there, there came a knock at the cabin door and an old hunter entered. I told him my story, but when I told him of the agonies I was suffering, he at last spoke.

"Why, God bless you, there is a simple remedy for that. Wait here and I will bring it to you within two hours."

He returned with a sack, and proceeded to render down some bear fat, from the bear he had killed just a few hours earlier.

"Drink this," he said, and so I down about a pint of bear fat. The following day all my pain had gone and my appetite returned.

Soon I was well enough to leave the cabin and travelled to Bozeman, where I met my friends who kept me company until my health was fully restored and I could return home to my daughter.

I am thankful to the members of my Expedition, who spent days searching for me. I am thankful to Judge Lawrence who made the offer of a reward, which brought Baronet and Prichette to my rescue.

My story ends here, but I believe that the day is not far distant when the wonders and grandeur of Yellowstone will be accessible to all who love nature.

I myself long to return to behold the spectacular sights of Yellowstone once more, and to experience their power to delight and transport the mind with their majesty and wonder.

SIX

THE LEGEND OF TSALI

It was the year of 1838, the gold rush had started and new rail roads were being built right across America.

Although he was growing older, Tsali was enjoying life on his small homestead. He'd made his home here in the foothills of the mountains, near the Little Tennessee River of North Carolina.

This was Tsali's home, a sacred place, the lands where he and his forefathers had lived and hunted for many years.

He was a Cherokee, but he and his family no longer lived in a teepee, but lived in much the same way as the white man. They lived in villages, sent their children to schools and even had a regular newspaper.

Tsali had built the log cabin on his homestead with his own hands, felling the tall trees, then hewing and shaping them to build a home for his wife and three sons.

Some years before, in 1831, the government, led by President Andrew Jackson, had signed the Indian Removal Act, which made it legal to 'resettle' the Cherokee. Resettling meant the Cherokee leaving their homes and moving out West of the Mississippi where they would be given new, unsettled lands.

Tsali knew that the leaders of the Cherokee nation had been fighting the Removal Act in the courts, so when, in the spring of 1838, his brother-in-law told him that thousands of soldiers were coming to round them up and take them to the West, Tsali still could not bring himself to believe such stories.

Yes, he'd heard himself called a 'savage', seen his Cherokee neighbours looted by the white men, but in his heart he still believed that the US government would send help and allow him to stay on the lands of his forefathers.

He'd heard that some of the local Indians had been permitted to stay, surely it was just a matter of time that the same agreement would be made for him and his peace-loving neighbours.

His ancestors bones lay in these hills and it was here that he wanted to be laid to rest, when his days on earth came to an end.

Tsali knew in his bones that there would not be many more winters until he too would lay with his ancestors - time was short for him to pass down to his sons the ancient Cherokee traditions and customs he had learnt from his father and grandfather.

"I'm too old to leave my home, to make a new start in a strange land," he thought to himself. "If I can live out my last years here and take care of my wife and family, I will have lived a good life and can die with honour."

Tsali loved nothing more than the joy of farming his small homestead and hunting to provide for his family. He hoped one day to see his sons and their families building their own homes in the lands of their forefathers.

But while Tsali was out hunting with his sons, teaching them the skills and knowledge of their tribe, history had set in motion events that were about to change his life forever.

7,000 soldiers were marching in to the area. They built stockades to use as holding pens for the Cherokees they planned to round up, before marching them West on what became known as the 'Trail of Tears'.

On the morning of 1st November 1838, Second Lieutenant, Andrew Jackson Smith, came to take Tsali and his family by force down to the stockade at Bushnell.

Stories differ as to what happened next, but somewhen on the march to the stockade, it's believed that one of the soldiers prodded Tsali's wife with his bayonet to get her to walk more quickly. Perhaps this disrespect for an older woman incensed Tsali, maybe the forced march away from his homestead was too much for him to bear.

A scuffle resulted, a loaded gun was discharged; in a few moments one soldier lay dead and another mortally wounded.

"Run!" cried Tsali, in his native tongue, as he helped his wife make her way into the woods at the foot of the mountains.

Tsali and his sons knew these hills well, even in winter, he believed he could hide his family here safely.

Over the next few days, more Cherokee joined them in the hills, hoping that they too might be allowed to stay in their beloved homeland.

While the Cherokee fled into the hills, Lieutenant Smith escaped on his horse. Just one week later, after receiving Lieutenant Smith's report, which made no mention of a soldier prodding Tsali's wife, General Scott gave the order. His order required that the Cherokee's involved in the incident must be hunted down and shot.

Tsali and his family remained hidden in the foothills for many days. Tsali had longed for his family to grow up in the lands of his ancestors and had hoped to live among them peacefully.

Yet, he knew that, whenever a man was killed, there must be a reckoning. It was a law as old as time itself. It was just a matter of waiting to see what would happen next.

Strangely enough, it would be a white man, who would act as a go-between between the Cherokee and the General.

Will Thomas, a white man, was the adopted son of Chief Drowning Bear, a Cherokee Indian.

Will Thomas knew that the white man could search for many months and never find Tsali and the other Cherokee fugitives.

"Don't send your soldiers," he asked General Scott, "let me go and reason with him."

As he made his way along the winding path up into the mountains, Will Thomas felt sure he could persuade Tsali to give himself up.

It wasn't long until Will was spotted by a Cherokee scout and word was passed to Tsali that a white man was approaching.

Cautious, Tsali looked out from his hiding place - recognising Will, he stepped out into the open.

"How do you do, my friend?" Will asked.

"I am fine, and you?" replied Tsali.

After greeting each other, they strolled together through the forest, until they came to sit around the camp fire.

"My friend, the General is angry. He has lost face because of what happened. Two of his soldiers lie dead. He has sent me with an offer for you."

Tsali listened intently.

"If you surrender, he will leave your people in peace, here in these hills, and not send them away to the West."

"But how can I trust the word of a white man?" asked Tsali.

"The General is a man of honour. Besides, you have no choice. If you do not agree, he will send his soldiers into the hills and hunt you and your family down. You will still be sent away, and many people will die. If you turn yourself in, there is still hope for your people."

"If this man can be trusted, what you say is wise and true. But first, let me spend some time with my wife and sons," replied Tsali.

And so Tsali, as is the way of any Cherokee preparing for death, spent his remaining time teaching his sons about the ways of his people in life and in death, so that they in turn would one day teach their sons and they in turn could teach their sons.

The time passed quickly, and it was time for Will to return with Tsali.

"My sons, there are many more things I could teach you. I have lived with honour. Now, I must teach you the hardest lesson of all, how to die with honour."

Saying goodbye to his family, Tsali walked out of the forest with Will Thomas, to face certain death in the white man's stockade.

As he stepped into the sunlight, he breathed deeply of the pure forest air one last time.

"Soon, I will lay with my ancestors. My soul will soon be resting in these hills," he thought. Then he strode, head held high, towards the stockade.

Standing as a prisoner before Colonel Foster, he was asked if he had any last request.

"Let me face death from the hands of my own people," he asked.

His wish was granted and three fellow Cherokees were chosen to be his executioners.

When they came with the blindfold, Tsali waved them away,

"No blindfold, I am not afraid of death."

"Ready, aim, fire!" Three shots rang out and Tsali fell to the ground. He had made the ultimate sacrifice for his people.

True to his word, the General allowed the people to stay in their beloved mountains, which is where they live to this day.

There's an Indian saying which says, "They are not dead who live in the hearts they leave behind."

Tsali lives today because he lives on in the hearts of his people and, it is said, that his spirit still walks the hills of his ancestors.

If you go hiking in the North Carolina foothills, you may catch a glimpse of a silent figure, head held high, silhouetted against the night sky.

SEVEN

THE FART IN THE DARK

It's not every day you turn thirteen. A teenager.

It's the age you get your passport. Not the one that lets you into other countries, and has that embarrassing picture of you with a neat parting in your hair and wearing clothes *only* Aunt Bertha could make.

You know the sort of thing; vomit coloured, hand knitted and with 'Super Boy' written in red on the front.

No, this is the passport to *growing up*. It's the invisible document that let's you be rude to your parents, stomp out of the room when you don't get your own way and refuse to eat Brussel sprouts, cabbage, broccoli or any vegetable except baked beans and sweetcorn (which is far too good to give up).

Mikey knew that this was all true, because he remembered when his sister, Angie, had turned thirteen.

She'd immediately changed from being an annoying girl who was still good fun and would play football with him, into a fearsome beast who shouted at Mom and Dad, had at least three strops a day and only left her room to watch the big TV or eat crisps. He'd endured two and a half years of that, and couldn't wait to be able to be a teenager himself.

Yes, he had high hopes that his thirteenth birthday was the passport to *fun*.

OK, it was a bit disappointing to be spending his special day away from home in Upton Snodsbury, but there'd been no way around it.

This camp out with school at North Piddle sounded great. Three nights under canvas with your mates; some kayaking and caving and abseiling; toasted marshmallows and ghost stories round the camp fire. Too good to be true, and not something to give up just for a birthday, not even a special one.

'We'll celebrate when you come back,' Mom had said.

'IF you come back,' Angie had added with a wicked smile. 'You've gotta go; three whole days without an annoying little baby in the house. Paradise.'

'And I promise to save you a piece of birthday cake … if I remember,' Dad added.

But there was never really any question of whether he would go or not.

So when Mikey woke up that warm June morning his mind went through a number of stages very quickly.

'Why am I lying on the floor?'

'Why is my ceiling flapping like it's made of canvas? (Oh, it is made of canvas, phew!)'

'Why are there five pairs of eyes staring at me, and five pairs of knees by my sleeping bag?'

'And while we're at it, isn't something supposed to be happening today?'

All of that took about a quarter of a second, and then it dawned on him.

It was his BIRTHDAY!

There, at the bottom of his bed, was a parcel wrapped up in red shiny paper. A couple of cards lay perched on top.

Mikey's best mate Andy was almost as excited as him.

'Come on, open your present. Your Mom gave it to me. I've had to keep it secret since we got on the bus.'

Cards first, one from Mom and Dad (and Angie, but Mikey knew that was Mom's writing), one from the rest of the boys in his tent.

Then the present. He tore off the paper and inside was a cardboard box. A post-it note was stuck to the top.

'You'll get your main present when you get home,' it read 'but thought you and your mates might like this for a midnight feast.'

Then underneath and written in big red letters it said, '*Don't tell your teachers!*'

And below that still in slightly smaller red letters, but underlined (twice), it said '*And if they find out, blame your Dad! Love Mom,*' followed by an embarrassingly long line of kisses.

Mikey undid the box, and his mates' eyes opened wide. The box was stuffed with every kind of scrumptious sweet a Mom who wanted to make her son sick could imagine.

It contained:

- six packs of Love Hearts
- twelve little tubes of Refreshers
- A giant plastic bag stuffed with flying saucers
- six sherbet dabs
- six packets of Parma violets (which Angie had dropped in when Mom wasn't looking)
- six mini bags of Haribo – the tangy ones which make your face screw up when you eat them
- twelve drumstick lollies

- eighteen Fruit Salads (with not an apple or strawberry in sight)
- twenty-four chewy snakes and
- thirty Cola Bottles. The sort you eat, not drink.

Thinking there's no time like the present and a lot could happen between now and midnight, Mikey was about to start dishing out the sweets.

Just then, the boys heard Mr Matthews' voice getting closer. 'Morning has broken,' he sang, rather painfully if we are to be honest.

'Quickly, hide them,' said Andy pointing at the sweets. He was the brains of the outfit, was Andy. Just in time, Mikey threw a crumpled sweatshirt over the box.

A head appeared inside the tent flap. 'Morning birthday boy,' it said, and withdrew rather quickly.

A tent which had had six sleeping boys in it all night is not necessarily the best place to put your head. Especially when the air outside is fresh and clear. Which certainly isn't the case when the odour of wet socks, dirty underwear, unwashed feet and too much fizzy drink has had a night to ferment.

The boys pulled on their clothes and headed out for breakfast. Mikey thought he'd better hide the box of sweets a little better, or even make them disappear altogether. And that was how it all started.

'I'll just test one,' he said to himself.

Well, what is better than a pre-breakfast aperitif of tangy Haribo washed down with a sherbet dab? He poured the Haribos into his mouth, like a thick, tangy milkshake (which is the only way to eat haribos. Stuff them into the mouth until no more fit, feel the multi-coloured dribble pour out your lips, chew, swallow and shiver.)

In fact, 'What is better than?' became Mikey's question of the day.

It went something like this …

What is better than … pancakes for breakfast, and being allowed to go for seconds AND thirds because it's your birthday?

What is better than … going back to your tent and celebrating your birthday by devouring a big bag of flying saucers with your mates?

What is better than … taking as many Cola Bottles as you can fit in your pockets to eat while waiting your turn on the abseiling cliff?

What is better than … sausage, chips and beans for lunch, and Andy gives you his beans as well because he's not hungry?

What is better than … two doughnuts, because the kitchen has some left over and you get first pick because you're the birthday boy?

What is better than … finishing off lunch with a couple of drumstick lollies?

What is better than … falling out of your kayak and swallowing half a lake? (Quite a lot, actually, especially when as soon as you get back in your boat, you fall out again, and swallow the rest.)

What is better than … Mom telling the camp it's your birthday and that chilli with garlic bread is your favourite dinner?

What is better than … double portions of apple pie with extra ice cream?

What is better than … the teachers organising a massive birthday cake for you to share with everybody?

What is better than … buying two cans of coke each and playing the 'burping alphabet' game with your mates?

What is better than … forgetting how to tell the time and having your midnight feast at seven 'o' clock at night?

What is better than … finishing your birthday by toasting marshmallows around the campfire?

Mikey sat beside the crackling flames. He felt very warm and very full.

The forked twig in his hand smouldered at the end where something pink and black was hanging loosely and threatening to fall off and into the fire. Beside him a can of lemonade fizzed gently, almost impossible to hear above the noise that surrounded the fire.

But the bubbles in the can were nothing compared to the bubbles frothing with even more fury inside him. Thundering, vibrating pockets of gas and air threatened at any moment to burst out, with who knew what consequences?

Chilli, garlic bread, combined with stinky lake water, ice cream and donuts, and a mountain of sugary sweets was wreaking havoc on Mikey's digestive system.

Mr Matthew's voice broke through his thoughts.

'Come on Mikey, eat up that marshmallow. You're getting left behind.'

The teacher was dancing towards him, a pair of shorts on his head and hairbands all the way up his arms. You couldn't argue with that.

With determination and trepidation, Mikey pushed the end of the stick towards his mouth. He genuinely feared that his insides were about to explode.

The trouble was, he didn't know whether everything would pour out of his mouth in a stream of sweet and sticky sick OR out of his other end in an explosive stream of smelly brown lava OR whether he would simply explode, and be left sitting there with his rib cage showing, his heart pumping forlornly and his friends covered in gory bits of Mikey's stomach contents.

Still, thought Mikey, when you are a teenager, you can deal with the challenges life throws your way. So, in went the marshmallow … and, much to his surprise, it went down and stayed there. At least, to begin with.

'OK, let's get to bed,' instructed Mr Matthews. But as everybody started to move off, Mikey was called in the other direction.

'You're Mom's on the phone,' said Miss Miller, who was helping out on the trip. 'But we need to go over to the offices, next to the dining hall to take the call.' And she gave a large wink to Mr Matthews.

'I wonder what's going on between those two?' thought Mikey, before a particularly violent pop in his tum directed his mind towards other things.

It would be great to talk to Mom, but Mikey was becoming aware that those internal bubbles were getting bigger, and noisier, and certainly a lot angrier.

'You OK?' asked Miss Miller in a whisper. Mikey nodded, but he wasn't. He was white and sweaty and feeling more than a little dodgy.

'Sorry miss, got to go,' he said, walking as quickly as a buttock clenching waddle would allow.

'I'll walk you up there,' Miss Miller's words were lost as his brain sought to remember the location of the nearest toilets. If only it would work as quickly as it had this morning, but now at least half of its processing power was focussed on keeping his butt closed.

'Right next to the dining hall,' they were the closest, but Mikey was really unsure he would make it now. He could feel little squeaks escaping from his lower quarters … step, squeak, waddle, squeak … he made his way to the dark square building in the distance more in hope than confidence. Never had the thought of a smelly communal toilet seemed so welcoming.

He was about three quarters of the way to the toilets, when Mikey knew he wouldn't make it. The battle with his insides was lost.

He still did not know how he would erupt, but erupt he definitely would. In fact, it would be such an eruption that the cloud of ash (or whatever) would probably encircle the planet for at least a week, causing planes all around the world to be grounded.

His stomach contracted and his throat and butt tightened more, held shut only by will power.

He pulled open the dining room door and stepped in the darkened room. Everything inside him finally relaxed, he let go of the tension and Mikey farted.

He farted like only a teenage boy stuffed with a week's worth of gas making food could do. It started as a loud explosion, so hard that Mikey feared his butt was about to form a new display on the dining room walls.

The explosion was followed by a long, but tuneful, raspberry which played every note in the musical scale. His bottom opened and closed like a trumpeter's lips playing a loud piece of jazz, and Mikey thought he might have invented a new kind of wind instrument.

The tune ended, but it wasn't finished there, three short encores followed, the last the longest of all. Rip, Rip, Riiiiiippppppsssschhhhhhh. Mikey's face relaxed in relief, but there was more to come. He could feel the pressure building up again.

There was no point denying the inevitable. Better out than in. He gave a little abdominal push and this time a deep rumble, like distant thunder, grumbled out. The room still had a hint of garlic in the air from dinner, but that was soon lost under the smell of a day's over-eating.

When that last rumble had stopped, three things happened all at once.

1) The lights went on …

2) Mikey saw that the room was full of people - his classmates, Mr Matthew, his parents (surprise!) and even his stinky sister.

3) The syllable 'Ha' (as in, Happy Birthday to You) burst out of thirty mouths, just as they'd been planning all day for Mikey's surprise party.

Mikey's classmates barely moved. Nor did Mr Matthews. They were turned to statues, silenced or petrified by his gaseous emissions.

As though coming back for one bow too many a little burp escaped his lips, and the last of the volcanic gas was gone.

Just then Mikey realised. It was his birthday. He could fart as much as he liked. He could burp as much as he liked and today, nobody could tell him off.

Just then, he felt another bubbling, swirling, gaseous explosion building up inside him.

With a smile on his face, the birthday boy bowed to his audience and let rip, "Ffffffffff…thththth….pffffftttttt!!!"

EIGHT

RED RED LIPS

It was his first night in the new house and Tyler was lying wide awake in bed. It had been a crazy busy day.

His room was filled with packing boxes of different sizes. The shadows on the wall and the sounds of the world outside his window seemed strange, but at least the bed was comfy and familiar.

Tyler lay staring at the ceiling. There was so much to think about.

Would he be able to make new friends? Would they accept him? How would his first day at school be?

As he lay there, with the thoughts running through his head, he thought he heard a scratching sound on the window.

There it was again!

"Scratch, scratch, scratch!"

Then, he heard a voice whispering on the other side of the window, "Do you know what I do with my red, red lips and my long, long fingers?"

Chilled to the bone, Tyler pulled his bedcovers up and put his head under the pillow. He tried to shut out the sound of the voice, by putting his hands over his ears.

But then, the voice beyond the window spoke again, "Do you know what I do with my red, red lips and my long, long fingers?"

"No!" He yelled, jumping out of bed, and pulling the bed covers with him, hiding under the bed.

Once more, the voice came, "Tyler, do you know what I do with my red, red lips and my long, long fingers?"

"No, and I don't want to know!" said Tyler, as loudly as he dared.

After what seemed like hours, Tyler finally fell asleep.

He awoke the next morning feeling tired and grouchy. Tomorrow was the start of school and his new life. Tonight he needed some sleep.

When he went to bed that night, he lay listening for a long while. Everything was silent.

"Maybe it was just a dream," he thought to himself.

Just as he was drifting off to sleep, he heard scratching at the window.

"Scratch, scratch, scratch!"

"Do you know what I do with my red, red lips and my long, long fingers?"

"No!" replied Tyler. He was tired and grouchy, he just needed some sleep.

"Tyler, would you like to know what I do with my red, red lips and my long, long fingers," came the voice at the window.

He ran to the window and found himself face to face with a wild woman, with long black hair hanging across her face and a deep scar across her cheek.

Desperate for sleep, Tyler answered.

"Alright then, just what is it that you do with your red, red lips and your long, long fingers?"

"I'll show you," came the reply.

For a moment, there was silence, then the woman brought her long, long finger up to her red, red lips and went,

"Blblblblblblblblblbblblblbl!"

(*Put your finger across your lips, breathe out a sound and move it up and down quickly to make this sound!*)

NINE

THE TALE OF SCREAMING WOOD

As night fell on the campsite, Jodie Williams shivered with excitement.

It was her birthday weekend and she'd managed to persuade her Dad to take her and three of her friends camping in the middle of the Screaming Wood. Not only that, but her Dad was *the* best at telling scary stories.

Jodie had now reached the perfect age (in fact, she was exactly the same age as you are now), and her Dad said she was old enough to hear some 'true' stories.

Of course, Jodie knew they were all made up, but the way he told them you'd swear they had actually happened.

"Well Jojo, …"

"Da-ad, I'm a whole year older now. Do you have to keep using that name? You used to call me that when I was a baby."

Jodie swore her Dad was hiding a smile as he looked at her.

"I'm sorry Jodie, but you're right. Now that you're not a little kid anymore, I need to give you a more grown up name. Jodie it is then."

The other girls were due to arrive at any minute, so Jodie and Dad set about putting up the tents – one big one for all the girls, and another smaller one for Dad.

"I don't mind you girls all sleeping in one tent, but it's on the condition that none of you leave the tent once we zip up for the night. Ok?"

"But what if one of us needs to go to the bathroom?"

Jodie's Dad had looked at her with one eyebrow raised.

"You're a big girl now kiddo, remember? If you need the bathroom you can use the bucket in the tent porch, but only little kids have to go in the middle of the night."

Not that she'd ever admit that to her Dad, but she felt a little scared at the thought of wandering through Screaming Wood in the middle of the night.

The beeping of a car horn made Jodie squeal with joy – a very un-grown up thing to do – as the other girls arrived.

Frankie, Jodie's BFF, had had dance practice that afternoon, so her Mom had agreed to bring the other two girls along with her while Jodie and her Dad got a head start on setting up their camp.

"Hi, Mrs Ricci."

Jodie liked Frankie's Mom, and greeted her excitedly.

"Hi Jodie, you've been busy. Are yours the only tents here?"

"Yes, but we'll be fine, Dad knows these woods really well and we're not far from home."

As Mrs Ricci pulled away, having dropped the girls off, she leaned out of her window and called out.

"Don't forget to look out for Bigfoot!"

Everyone laughed as they set to help putting up the tent, then organising their belongings just the way they wanted them. Then they gathered around the camp fire that Jodie's Dad had got going.

Dad handed out some long sticks and a handful of big, fluffy marshmallows each, along with some chocolate-covered graham crackers and sat himself down on a rock.

"Find yourselves somewhere comfy to sit girls, the ground is pretty flat here. You can grab your sleeping bags to keep you warm if you don't mind them smelling of smoke."

Bex and Anna, Jodie's almost-best friends, threw down their sweaters to sit on, and immediately began piercing the marshmallows with their sticks, eager to start toasting them as soon as possible to make some delicious s'mores. Jodie and Frankie were choosier, searching for the perfect spot.

"Here! I found a great place to sit. Look Frankie!"

Jodie scuffed her toe into an indentation in the dry ground, where the base was totally smooth and flat and the sides were slightly raised.

"This. Is. Perfect!"

The two girls settled down side by side in their little nook, and as the smell of toasted mallows and happy munching filled the air, Jodie remembered what Frankie's Mom had said.

"Dad, what did Mrs Ricci mean about Bigfoot?"

Mr Williams was quiet for a moment as he rolled the hot marshmallow around his mouth, then he slid off the rock and onto the ground, so he was eye-level with the girls, and leant back against his former seat.

Jodie knew that face, that was his story face! She linked arms with Frankie and smiled excitedly at the other two girls.

As he looked from girl to girl, the firelight played on his face, casting shadows that danced on his cheeks and seemed to fill his eyes with tiny flickering flames.

"Once upon a time ..."

Jodie groaned.

"Dad, we're not kids anymore. We don't want fairy tales."

Mr Williams looked serious, as he pulled another marshmallow off his stick with his teeth.

"Believe me Jodie, this is NO fairy tale."

The flames in the fire seemed to grow still as Mr Williams began, his face shrouded in the shadows.

"It was a long time ago, in these very woods, that Bigfoot was first seen in these parts. These woods weren't always known by the name of Screaming – no, many years ago this exact same place was known as Redblood Forest.

The name came from the river that runs through the middle. Every full moon the river ran red, the water rising as if the blood of a thousand animals .."

He stopped and looked at each of the girls in turn.

".. had spilled into it, causing it to burst its banks and stain the surrounding area red.

At first, the locals thought it was coming from a disused mine some miles upstream, but when they got inspectors in to check, the place was completely abandoned and there was nothing there which would account for the water turning red.

Nobody realised at first that it only happened at full moon, until a few years ago, when a man decided to live in the forest for a few weeks, to see if he could find out what was causing the crimson floods.

He pitched his tent a little way from the river."

Mr Williams stopped talking suddenly, as if he had heard something. Frankie and Jodie snuggled up closer, while Bex ran into the tent to bring her sleeping bag out, and she and Anna wrapped it around their shoulders like a blanket.

The temperature hadn't changed, but suddenly, the girls felt colder.

Mr Williams looked around him: he looked at the trees, and the ground, and further out, through the trees as if he was trying to see what lay beyond the tall fragrant pines.

A shiver ran down Jodie's spine, as if someone had reached out a finger and drawn a line from her neck to her waist. She looked around quickly, but there was no-one there. She looked back at her Dad.

"It was here, wasn't it? Where the man set up his tent?"

Her Dad nodded slowly, still looking out through the trees before continuing.

"Yes, in this very clearing. It was far enough away from the river that, if the levels did rise, it wouldn't flood his tent, but close enough that he could hear … well, so he could hear … the screams."

The four friends shuddered, and strained their ears to see if they could hear anything. The moon was rising, and it cast an opaque glow over the little group. Jodie spoke to her Dad, wishing he would stop looking off through the trees as it was making her nervous.

"What happened, Dad? To the man?"

Mr Williams shook himself, like a dog that's come out of the water, and turned his attention back to the girls. He smiled, but Jodie frowned – his smile didn't quite reach his eyes.

"He set up his tent, and for the next couple of weeks he slept during the day so he could stay awake all night, which is when folk had said river water color changed to red. Every day, when he would wake from his sleep, he would tie one end of string to a big rock …"

The four girls turned their gaze upon the rock Mr Williams had been sitting on.

" … and he would mark his trail with the string, letting it out as he walked, to make sure he had a way of finding his tent again should he get lost in the dark.

Once the sun goes down, all parts of the forest look the same, and it's easy to lose your bearings and be lost for days … or forever.

One night, about four weeks or so after the last blood river, John Clarke - the man who had set himself the task of discovering the truth behind the mystery – woke up to find a bright light shining into his tent.

His first thought was that someone had stumbled across his camp and was shining a torch in his face, but then he realised that it was the moon – big, and bright, so bright that it lit up the entire forest.

It was a full moon, and John was grateful for the extra light as he once again made his way toward the river.

Once again he tied the string around the rock, and began to make his way through the forest, walking slowly, ever so slowly, the moonlight glittering through the trees, until he could hear the sound of rushing water and knew he was near the river.

As John got closer, the noise got louder and louder, and then suddenly there was a high-pitched scream … a sound so terrifying, so petrifying, that they say John's hair turned white with the shock!

As he turned around, he caught sight of a huge creature, standing at least 10 feet tall, covered in thick, long hair and with the biggest feet he had ever seen.

A cloud passed in front of the moon, but just before it did, John got a glimpse of the creature snarling at him as it came towards him. The fright was too much for John, and he fainted, falling face down on the riverbank."

The girls were silent as Mr Williams paused to stoke up the fire, which had grown smaller as he had talked. Jodie shivered, and snuggled in closer to Frankie. Even in the orange glow of the campfire, she could see that the other girls' faces were pale.

Mr Williams leaned towards the girls and continued in a lower voice.

"When John woke up, he was all alone on the riverbank. He was cold, and wet, but he was alive. He looked about him slowly, waiting to feel the pain, but none came, and as he got to his knees, John realised that the creature had gone, and as he stood up he even wondered whether he had imagined it all.

The sky had grown cloudy, and there was barely any moonlight by the time he started his way back to the camp. Feeling his way along the string guide he had set up earlier, John eventually found his tent and started a fire to warm himself. His wet clothes began to dry and he picked up his diary to record the night's events.

Exhausted, John dampened the fire and zipped himself into his tent, knowing that he would fall into a deep sleep. But as he lay there, he began to doubt himself. Did he really see the creature? Had he actually heard that blood curdling scream?

Maybe the tiredness of the past few weeks had caught up with him. After all, if the creature had been real, why was he, John, still alive? He laughed to himself as he turned over in his sleeping bag, and fell asleep.

After a fitful sleep, John awoke, convinced he had imagined the whole episode. Feeling refreshed and with just a few hours to go until sundown, he took his mirror out of his backpack, set it up on the rock, and poured some drinking water into a small bowl.

Having spent weeks living in a tent, he was looking decidedly scruffy. That beard had to go. He splashed water on his face then bent to look in the mirror, horror filling his veins like ice-cold blood. His face was encrusted with … he didn't like to even think what it must be.

His mind thought back to the night before, and the events replayed in his mind … the terrifying scream, the creature, and falling … falling onto the ground.

He remembered waking up, feeling cold and wet. And yet, the river bank had been dry as he'd walked along it, so why was it wet when he woke?

His eyes widened, he began to run, stumbling through the dense trees, following the string which was still up from the night before, heading towards the sound of the rushing river. But as he got closer, his feet began to sink into the mud, water seeping into his boots, the ground sodden and boggy.

And red ... very very red.

When John didn't return home when he was supposed to, a search party was sent to look for him, and they found this clearing, the clearing you are sitting in now, with nothing left in it but a torn, tattered tent, and John's journal – the one where he had been writing about his search for the truth.

A few years later, a construction company wanted to build holiday cabins here, but no matter how many times they flattened the ground, every time there was a full moon huge footprints would appear on the ground, big, deep, too big to have been made by any human or animal.

Legend has it that, with every full moon, the footprints grew bigger ... and bigger ... and bigger.

The owner was called in and, like John, he decided to spend a few nights in the forest to get to the truth".

Jodie looked at her father. "So, what happened, Dad? Why didn't they build the cabins?"

Mr Williams stood up and slowly walked around the clearing.

"Because, just like John, the owner disappeared. His last planned night here there was a full moon, and in the morning ... he was gone. All that was left was a trail of giant footprints on the ground that led down towards the river."

The girls were quiet, and then Jodie started laughing when she looked at her Dad's face.

"Da-ad ... you almost made us believe you then!"

Bex looked from one to the other.

"So, it didn't happen then?"

Mr Williams held his flashlight up to his chin so his face looked ghostly and let out a sinister laugh.

"Mooohahahahahaha … who knows? Now go to bed, before Big Foot gets yo—"

Mr Williams stopped dead, and looked from his daughter to the ground where she and Frankie had been sitting.

"There … there's a dent. Look … a big dent," he said in a hushed voice.

Jodie laughed and smacked her Dad playfully on the arm.

"It wasn't us, we're not that heavy! It was already there."

"Ssshhhh..!" urged Mr Williams.

As the four girls and Mr Williams looked down at the place where the friends had been sitting, Jodie realised.

"Oh my gosh … it's a, it's a big, giant footprint!"

Mt Williams looked up at the sky. "And a full moon …"

His voice trailed off …

Just then, they heard a snapping of twigs underfoot and saw an enormous, dark shadow emerging from the forest.

"Let's get out of here," cried Jodie, as they all began to run.

TEN

THE OLD COWBOY

An old cowboy strolled into the town saloon.

"Give me a whiskey!"

The locals watched him, but no-one said a word.

The first thing they noticed was that his cowboy hat was made of paper.

On closer inspection, they could see that his shirt and pants were made from paper too.

In fact, everything he wore was made of paper.

Everyone shifted in their chairs nervously. Who was this stranger?

It was as if the sheriff sensed that something was awry, because at that very moment, he walked into the bar and strode right up to the stranger.

"You're under arrest!" he said.

"What for?" asked the stranger.

"For rustling,' replied the sheriff.

ELEVEN

A THIEF IN CAMP

Life doesn't always turn out the way you expect.

Sometimes, plans that seemed like the best idea ever don't turn out the way you thought they would.

They may seem to be the greatest idea since somebody chucked some milk, flour and eggs into a bowl and invented pancakes, but somehow they don't end up tasting that good.

One day, you're planning a great sleepover at Anna's house, the next you wake up covered in itchy spots.

Or you've had your eye on that sparkly top for weeks, and Mom finally takes you to the shops. You try it on and it makes you look about five years old.

Which, when you're a lot older than five years old, is something you absolutely do not want to happen.

And that, reflected Jo, was how it was now.

It had all started a year ago when, bursting with excitement, the plan had seemed perfect.

Her parents ran a small business in a village in the south of England, about an hour's drive from London.

But their business was about to get very large, because Jo's parents were about to launch Doggy Don't Don't. Which is, as we all know, the biggest advance in canine care since somebody invented Doo Doo bags.

Before that, they'd made Doggy Doo Doo, those little plastic bags dog owners use to pick up their pets' poo poo. Their catchphrase was 'A Doo Doo deals with any Pooch's Poo Poo.'

They made Doo Doo's in pink and grey and black, baby powder scented and mint scented and even 'Vanilla, Vanilla: the Smell of Poop Killer'.

But, let's face it, even if your bag is purple with green spots and smells of maple syrup or vanilla, picking up dog poo is still a pretty yucky job. Especially if it's a runny one.

"Yuk!" Jo shivered just thinking about it.

It had all started one day, when she'd been walking to school in Higher Dingworthy with her Mom.

That's when they saw a little old lady trying to collect her Jack Russell's you-know-whats. She was bent over, trying her absolute best to get down to ground level, but she just couldn't reach it.

Jo's Mom saw she had a packet of their Doggy Doo Doos – the yellow ones scented with spring daffodil and banana - so she offered to help.

'Can I give you a hand?' Mom asked.

'Tuesday, I think,' replied the old lady, still bent over.

'No dear, if you give me the Doo Doo, I'll pick it up for you,' said Mom, a little more loudly and a lot more slowly.

'Porridge, toast and marmalade, with a nice cup of tea. Not that it's any of your business,' replied the old lady.

In the end she got the message, handed over a bright yellow Doo Doo bag and Mom got to work. The reason the old lady had found it hard to hear Mom wasn't that she was deaf (well, she might have been) but that there was a great big lorry next to them.

The lorry had a long black tube poking out of its side, which was exploring a hole in the road. A heavy manhole cover sat next to it, and the hole let out a very dodgy smell.

The rumble of the lorry's engine mixed with the glugging of the sewage. It was sucking up the stinky stuff from the hole in the ground and pumping it safely away into the lorry's tank.

'I could do with one of those,' said the little old lady with a smile, nodding towards at the noisy truck.

And that was that. Those seven innocent words were the reason that Jo was sitting on a rock by a stream in Texas, USA, feeling rather sad and lonely.

Mom, you see, was nothing if not a get on and go person. A bit of an entrepreneur.

She saw the potential solution for dog owners around the world and within six months the Doggy Don't Don't (as in, don't bend over, and don't get a nose full of stinky smell) was born.

About the size of a toaster, this invention took the back ache out of clearing up after your dog. And the risk of a smelly hand.

When Rover did his business, you simply unhooked the Don't Don't and pressed a button. Out popped a long tube with a wide end covered with a Doo Doo.

You placed it close to the disgusting droppings, pressed a second button and, with a whoosh, the poo – however runny – was sucked up into the bag, and then along the tube and into the Doo Doo holder at the top.

This was covered with a larger Doo Doo bag, which collected all the little Doo Doo bags and when you got to a *Dog Poo Bin* you simply took out the larger bag and *threw it in*. (Dad thought there was another catchphrase there, but Mom told him you can have too much of a good thing.)

Now, Mom and Dad were bringing their Don't Don't to America. They'd already spent six weeks travelling round the country, showing it off. At first, Jo had trailed along with them. The first few weeks had been great fun but the next part of their journey would be all about contract signing and loads of boring stuff like that.

Way back, six months ago, Mom and Dad had known that these two weeks of their trip would be rather dull, so had suggested booking Jo into to an American Summer Camp.

It had sounded like a great plan. What could be more fun than that?

Quite a lot, Jo was discovering.

There was nothing really bad about it. It was just that Jo had dreamed of two weeks of kayaking, midnight feasts and fun with new found friends. But the girls in her lodge didn't seem very friendly.

The three girls, Sandy, Layla and Mickey all came from the same school, and knew each other really well. They weren't mean to Jo, they just sort of forgot she was there.

And as for midnight feasts, not a chance. These girls were all Miss Goody Goody Six Shoes (there being three of them).

Once the teacher – sorry, counsellor (what a silly name for a teenager not much older than her, thought Jo) put the lights out, they were all asleep in five minutes.

"Boring!" thought Jo.

And so, three days into her not very exciting adventure, Jo couldn't wait for the next eleven days to pass so her parents could collect her and they could continue their journey, selling Don't Don'ts to America.

'Still', she thought, 'at least I've got my bag of crisps to look forward to'.

It was a bit sad really, getting excited about a bag of crisps, but that was how far Jo had fallen. Except they were not called crisps in America, they were called chips.

'What a stupid name', she thought. In England chips were lovely, hot, sticks of potato, fried and covered in salt and vinegar and tomato ketchup.

Except, in this country, chips were fries and crisps were chips. Mind you, that didn't mean that they were anything but delicious.

Jo had found a flavour she especially liked, which she couldn't get at home. Jalapeño. Spicy and shivery. Dad had bought them at the airport when they landed. It had all started as a joke when Dad insisted everybody try one. What a happy accident that was. They were delicious. Jo had bought several packets to take along to camp with her.

'Serendipity,' said Mom. But she often said things like that and it was best to just ignore her or she'd go into a long explanation of the meaning of the word, and mention it at least once an hour for the next three days.

Not all of Dad's experiments in cuisine worked as well as the Jalapeño crisps. Their first night, as they'd sat down in the hotel restaurant, he'd ordered Fried Okra. Apparently, that was a Texan treat. 'Ladyfinger,' said Dad randomly.

Jo remembered Dad's face as he took too large a mouthful. It had started blank, but as the pungent flavour seeped into his taste buds, his eyes had widened. Then he'd bitten into the soggy interior, like taking a mouthful of wet sand on the beach. He'd shuddered in horror. Okra tasted like mushy, rotten flesh.

Jo smiled, then realised she was doing it again. Dreaming of getting out of this camp, rather than keeping busy.

'Super Sunshine Camp, the Perfect Summer For Six To Sixteen Year Olds (siblings half price)' read the banner on their web page.

Back in February, with icy rain pouring down outside, the photos of sunny lakes and smiling kids kayaking across a picture perfect lake had seemed so appealing.

But now, she was faced with the reality of several boring days before she was back with her parents.

Jo sighed and headed for the lodge. She pushed through the door – the others had gone somewhere, without her as usual – and she went to get her chips.

They weren't there. Jo opened her small wooden locker. She checked under the bed and looked inside her case. But the crisps weren't there. The chips were down. It was her last bag, and it was gone.

When you're feeling upset, silly things can take on huge importance. Suddenly a bag of crisps became as important as the Crown Jewels.

She searched and hunted and peered into every corner. But the Jalapeño Chips, the best crisps in all America, had, quite simply, disappeared.

As she was puzzling over this, the door opened, and in walked the other three girls. Layla, who slept in the bed next to her, screwed up a crinkly bag and threw it into the bin.

'Hi, Jo,' she said. 'Having fun?'

Before Jo could reply, another of her room mates, Sandy, put her hands on her head in a dramatic fashion.

'Disaster!' she cried, 'I've left my baseball cap by the lake.'

And with much giggling the girls turned and left the lodge. Jo headed straight to the bin. She took out the chip bag, unravelled it and read the words on the shiny paper. 'Jalapeño flavor' they said, in big red letters, the 'l's made of green jalapeño peppers.

Jo was furious as the terrible crime to which she had fallen victim to became clear.

'She stole my crisps!'

The next morning came and Jo was still feeling angry with Layla. In fact, she was cross with all three of the girls.

'Time for breakfast, let's go!' Mickey, the final girl in the lodge, had said, and the three friends had headed out. They hadn't actually said she couldn't go with them, but it seemed clear to Jo that they didn't want her along.

Layla was pretty untidy, and on her unmade bunk Jo saw a book, 'Mallory Towers' one of Enid Blyton's stories about some girl's adventures in an English boarding school.

'Hmm,' thought Jo, 'You're more interested in England than you let on.'

There were also some scrunched up pyjamas and a bar of Almond Joy laying on the rumpled covers.

'Not much joy in that,' thought Jo. She hated nuts. They made her lips swell up and if she ate too many they caused her to vomit wildly.

She hated candy bars as well. (They didn't taste the same as the chocolate in England and it made her feel homesick.) When she came to think of it, Jo thought, she hated everything American.

With a slam of the door behind her, she headed off to the cafeteria. It was pancakes, drizzled with maple syrup, for breakfast. Well, maybe she didn't hate everything American after all.

In fact, Jo didn't hate the pancakes so much that she had a second portion. By the time she arrived back at the lodge the other three girls were already there and it was obvious there was something wrong.

'Nobody's been in, so you must have put it somewhere else,' Sandy was saying.

'Yeah Layla, you are kinda messy,' Mickey added her opinion.

'It was on my bed. I left my book, my pajamas and my candy bar on the top of it. Hey, Jo, did anybody come in while we were at breakfast?'

'No,' said Jo, surprised to have been spoken to. 'I was here by myself, and I followed you about five minutes later.'

The other three girls shared meaningful looks, but said no more. It was clear to Jo that they all thought they knew where the Almond Joy bar had gone.

The activity for the morning was kayaking and the instructor told everyone to get into pairs. Sandy, Mickey and Layla moved together, and Jo was left alone. Again.

'I'll go with the English girl,' Layla finally said. She didn't even say Jo's name.

Let's just say it was a bit awkward. Being in a boat with someone who stole your Jalapeño crisps – sorry, Jo rebuked herself, chips – didn't make for the best of atmospheres. Especially, from Layla's point of view, when you were pretty sure your partner was responsible for the loss of a much loved almond joy bar.

Eventually, Jo decided to break the ice.

'I didn't take your bar,' she said.

It was the worst thing possible to say.

'Nobody said you had,' snapped Layla from behind her. A sudden splash and burst of speed told Jo that this conversation was best left there.

The rest of the morning was almost fun. The sun shone, the water was refreshing and the instructor loved nothing more than a good splash. Everybody had a great time. Everybody, that is, except two girls from different sides of the Atlantic who sat silently and grumpily in their kayak.

When lunchtime beckoned and the kayaks had been dragged onto the little beach beside the lake, Jo rushed off. She wanted to be away from the three girls as quickly as was possible.

In fact, by the time Layla, Mickey and Sandy got back to the hut, still dripping, Jo had hung her wet clothes up to dry outside, got changed and headed for a quiet corner to eat a sandwich and read by herself.

She got as far as getting her phone out and preparing to text Mom to come and collect her, but she knew that this could result in them losing their contract to supply America with Doggy Don't Don'ts.

She may be suffering, but, she told herself, with some stiff British upper lip, she could see it through. After all, there was only ten days to go … just ten!

A few minutes later, her resolve was put to the test. As she headed back to the lodge, hoping the others were out playing or having their own lunch, she saw a sight which brought tears to her eyes. Her clothes, which had been so neatly hung up, were thrown all over the ground. Worst of all, her favourite T Shirt, the one with purple unicorns and the slogan 'My Mom went to Fairyland and All I Got were these Fake Unicorns' on the front, was gone.

Now that was cruel. Very cruel. Jo hadn't taken Layla's chocolate bar and, even if she had, then she didn't deserve this.

Suddenly, Jo hoped the others were inside the lodge. She was ready for a fight.

But when she opened the door, it seemed like there had been one already. Inside the hut, the pages of Mallory Towers fluttered in the breeze brought in through the open window. They were everywhere.

Jo slumped on her bed, but the pages kept blowing around and annoying her. In the end, she decided to collect them up. Jo had collected half a handful when the door to the lodge opened.

'What have you been doing to that book?' Mickey asked.

'That's just plain nasty,' whispered Sandy. They all assumed Jo was tearing it to pieces.

Layla just stared at the fluttering pages. And Jo was so cross at their reaction that she couldn't find the words to explain that she was clearing up the mess, not making it.

The evening passed in silence. Next morning the three girls went off to breakfast, leaving Jo behind.

"If they want Mallory Towers, I'll give them something to think about!" thought Jo.

She'd read some fiendish stories about what the girls did in their dorm rooms at boarding school. It was about time she used her knowledge to good effect.

Grabbing some bright yellow unscented Doggy Doo Doo bags, she snuck out of the cabin and looked around for something stinky to fill them with. Just a few steps from the cabin, she found some animal droppings that fitted the bill perfectly. Soon she had three bags, filled with stinky poo, and she was ready to carry out her plan.

Hiding the Doo Doo bags under the girls pillows, all she had to do was wait until nightfall.

All through night, she could hear the girls tossing and turning in their beds.

"I couldn't sleep a wink, something in this cabin stinks!" said Sandy, looking straight at Jo.

"Enough's enough," thought Jo, "It must be time for breakfast waffles," and headed out the door for breakfast.

After Jo left the girls made their beds and discovered the mean trick that Jo had played on them all.

"If she thinks she can trick us, she's got another thing coming. We'll show her!" said Mickey.

And so, a little bleary-eyed, the girls set about to set a trap that would really teach Jo a lesson.

When she returned from breakfast, full of waffles and maple syrup, Jo was humming a little song to herself.

As she walked up the cabin steps and opened the door, she was not prepared for what happened next.

"Sploooosh!"

A bucket filled with gloopy wallpaper paste, which the girls had carefully perched on the top of the door, which they'd left slightly ajar, tipped down, all over her head.

As she stood there dripping wet and covered in big splodges of the sticky paste, she spotted the faces of her three tormentors peering over the edge of a bed.

It was time to end this once and for all.

Everything happened in seconds. Each girl grabbed a pillow and soon feathers were flying across the room. Accusations flew almost as fast as the feathers.

"Why you …" started Jo, "mean-faced, thoughtless, crisp stealing ratbags!"

"Why you," said Layla, "snob-faced, book-ripping, candy stealing poo-face!"

It was at that exact moment that Sally, their camp counsellor, walked through the door.

'What on earth is going on? Thing don't seem too friendly,' she remarked, in what was probably the understatement of the week.

It was like popping a cork out of a bottle of the fizziest lemonade. All the bubbling anger that had been stopped up in the room burst out.

'She ripped up my book,' shouted Layla

'Pffft', started Jo, spitting out a handful of sticky feathers, 'she ruined my T-shirt.'

'She stole my candy bar,' said Layla.

'She ate my crisps,' roared back Jo.

'Chips!' screamed the other three girls.

'And,' muttered Jo with feeling, 'they were Jalapeño flavour.'

'She did all that for no reason,' balled Layla, close to tears.

'They stole my food,' countered Jo with pent up fury.

'We didn't!' responded all the girls together.

At last, everyone went quiet.

The camp counsellor had listened to all the accusations. Then she took a good long look at the open window.

'I might have the answer here,' she paused, thinking about what to do next.

'But first, let's clean up all this mess.'

The girls groaned, cleaning up would take ages.

Then, Jo had an idea.

'We can use the Doggy Don't Don't. It's perfect!'

They pulled it from the packaging, plugged it in and, within moments, the Don't Don't and its gobbling tube had the cabin clean as a whistle.

All that was left was for Jo to have a shower to wash off all the gloopy mess and feathers, and all the girls were ready.

'Now, off you go to your afternoon activities,' said Sally, 'and leave this to me.'

Two hours later the girls arrived back at their lodge. They were still barely talking to each other.

'I think it's time we watched a movie,' said Sally.

Everyone groaned. No-one was in the mood for a movie.

But then Sally held up her phone. Feeling intrigued, the girls gathered round.

They were surprised to see that the movie was of their hut, and there, right in the middle of the floor, sat a bowl of popcorn.

'I'll fast forward a bit, everything will make sense in a minute or two,' said Sally. 'I left my phone on record, and set it up over there.' She pointed to a shelf opposite the window.

About twenty minutes into the recording the phone picked up a rattling sound. Then a grey, stripy, furry animal poked its nose through the window. It had a sniff, and then came in. Straight to the popcorn.

Watching a racoon eating a bowl of popcorn is enough to make anybody smile, even enemies forced together at summer camp.

Bits of popcorn flew everywhere. They stuck to its fur, they became glued to its snout, and were spread all over the floor. Soon everyone was laughing.

'I think we've found our culprit,' said the counsellor.

She pointed to a sign above the window: 'Keep Closed,' it read, 'Raccoons Like To Visit.'

'Oh dear,' said Jo.

'Whoops,' said Layla.

They all felt so foolish that they'd jumped to conclusions without talking to each other first.

Layla was first to speak.

'We wanted to make you welcome, but you seemed so sad,' she said. 'I even got Mallory Towers from the camp library so I could learn about English girls. I'm sorry you've had such a horrible time'

'I'm so sorry I blamed you for taking my crisps … chips' Jo said before the others could correct her. 'By the way, I'm allergic to nuts,' she said quietly.

Then they looked at each other, and four wide, cheesy smiles broke out across four happy faces and it was group hug time.

After that, you couldn't separate the four of them.

The next few days went by so quickly, until they all said a tearful goodbye at the end of camp.

A month later and Layla Mitchell was walking home with her dog and a little bag of doggy doo, full of – well, you can guess. Both she and her puppy had enjoyed a good stroll through the park.

On the front step, there was a parcel waiting for her. A square one. All the way from England. Inside was a bright box with 'Doggy Don't Don't' brightly printed on its cover, next to a smiling dog and her owner. A note was attached.

'This will make taking your puppy for a walk easier,' it read, under a hand drawn picture of a girl walking her dog. 'Can't wait for when you come to stay with us in England. Love, your BFF, Jo.'

Layla smiled. In just a few months, she was going to fly over and visit Jo.

She stopped for a moment and thought about how they'd become friends. Then she laughed to herself. She was very thankful indeed that there were no racoons in England, where she was headed!

TWELVE
A CRICK IN THE BACK

There was once an old man who loved to go out canoeing on the lake.

However, each time he bent down to pick up the canoe paddle, he'd get a painful crick in his back.

Eventually he went to see the doctor, who gave him some rather unusual advice.

"When this happens again, grab the paddle with both hands. Place the base of the paddle on the ground and pull yourself up the length of the paddle."

Sure enough, next time the old man went out canoeing, he bent down and felt the crick in his back.

Remembering the doctors words, he grabbed the paddle, placed the base on the ground and pulled himself up along the length of the paddle.

He beamed with joy as he was finally upright, most happy to discover that he was up the paddle without a crick.

THIRTEEN

QUEST FOR BIGFOOT

Chapter 1

Mum had always told him to follow his dreams. But dad had always said he should get what he called a 'decent' job.

"Something steady, like plumbing or carpentry, or maybe a mechanic. People are always gonna need to have toilets unblocked or get their cars fixed. Of course, I'd much rather you were a doctor or a law—", but one look from Mum had been enough to remind Ryan's dad not to go there, the implication being that Ryan just wasn't smart enough for that kind of job.

Mum always said, "You do what'll make you happy Ry, that's the true definition of success in my book."

So, Ryan had followed his dreams, and once he'd finished school he'd enrolled in college to study anthropology.

He'd always been interested in human behaviour, and spending his days learning how mankind had evolved didn't feel like work to him, he loved every moment of it. Long after his college books had been closed at night, Ryan would study his favourite subject of all – Bigfoot.

For as long as he could remember, he'd been fascinated with the legend.

It was a legend that had many different names: Bigfoot, Sasquatch, Yeti, and maybe even the Abominable Snowman, but Ryan could see nothing abominable about it – to him, Bigfoot was a beautiful creature who had simply been misunderstood by the men who now hunted for it.

Chapter 2

His fascination (some would even call it an obsession) began when he'd gone camping with his dad when he was just 12 years old.

His mum had called it 'bonding time' for them both. He and his father had headed off into the woods many miles from home. While there they'd met up with Peter and Parker, who were also away for a dad and son camping trip.

Sitting around the campfire on the first night, Peter, the dad, had told tales of a creature who was so big and so hairy, that people were terrified of him.

"He's nearly 10 feet tall, some people say, and hairy, so hairy, just like a gigantic ape. He leaves footprints far bigger than any human's – at least 24 inches long. That's why he's called Bigfoot."

"And he eats people!" shouted Parker, a young boy of around seven, who was clearly enjoying the story and just wanted to join in.

Peter laughed. "I'm not sure that he eats anyone, but they do say he's been spotted in these very woods, and that if you listen carefully you can hear him talking or chattering with his Bigfoot family."

Ryan had been listening intently.

"He talks?"

Peter nodded.

"Not any language that you or I could understand, but he chatters, a sound somewhere between ape and human."

That night, Ryan slept soundly, his dreams filled with images of an enormous creature who was half man, half beast. But instead of scenes of horror, as Parker had excitedly suggested, these were happy dreams of whole families of these elusive creatures, living together in the wilderness.

The next night, as Ryan lay in his sleeping bag and his father snored gently beside him, he heard it. It sounded like a quiet but steady hum of noise … no, not noise, a chatter, like a far off conversation, where you can't quite make out the words.

At once Ryan knew exactly what he was hearing, there wasn't any other sound on earth like it.

Creeping quietly out of the tent, Ryan ventured into the woods alone. Although he knew Bigfoot was about – after all, he had heard him – he wasn't afraid.

And that's when he saw it; a single footprint, huge and deep, as though it was made by something, or someone, extremely large and very heavy.

At that moment, Parker's words came flooding back to him, "He eats people!" Even though he didn't believe it was true, the sheer size of the footprint had surprised him. In all his dreams, he hadn't been prepared for this.

The sounds of the forest echoed through the dark and, for one moment, he allowed the fear that had been knocking at the door of his mind to step inside. Instead of pushing forward to find Bigfoot, Ryan turned and ran, back to the safety of the tent.

The next morning, he felt ashamed for allowing the fear to control him. Vowing to have one more go to find Bigfoot, he dragged his father into the woods to show him the footprint, but the ground was soft and wet from the overnight rain, and any trace of Bigfoot had vanished.

That one encounter had set Ryan's future career in motion, and nothing was going to stop him in his quest for Bigfoot, but unlike others who wanted to hunt down the elusive Yeti, Ryan wanted to study them, befriend them. He even dreamed that, one day, he might live among them for a while.

Chapter 3

Ryan's hard work paid off, and to his delight he received a grant from the 'Bigfoot Exploration Society' to fund his studies.

Ryan had set up home with his girlfriend, Lou. Lou was a nice girl, but she had no interest in his fascination with Yetis.

"I don't know why you have to have so many books and pictures of them everywhere," she'd said. "They look like such stupid, clumsy creatures!"

Ryan found this hurtful, but he was convinced that one day he'd prove her wrong and that, she too, would become a Bigfoot believer.

It was just an ordinary Wednesday evening, when, at last, recognition of his work came when he received a telephone call.

After that phone call, Ryan thought that Lou would have to take him seriously. He waited impatiently for her to come home so he could tell her his news.

"Lou, come and sit down, I've got some seriously exciting news. I had a phone call today from—"

"Ryan, I really need a shower. Can it wait?"

So Ryan had to sit on his news for a bit longer. When Lou had finished in the bathroom, Ryan sat her down, handed her a cup of tea, and told her about his phone call.

"The Bigfoot Exploration Society called me, Lou. There's been sightings of Bigfoot at a ghost town on the coast, up in Alaska, and they want me to fly out there and verify the claims! This could be the big break I'm looking for. If I find it, I could really make a name for myself."

Lou rolled her eyes.

"Yeah, or it could break you when you get there and find it's just another crackpot making up stories. Seriously, Ryan, grow up! Only little kids believe in Bigfoot."

She paused for a moment, before she spoke again.

"If you swan off to Alaska, I won't be here when you come back. You know I mean it!"

Ryan was crushed. Lou had always listened to him before, and seemed to go along with his dreams. He was only just beginning to realise that it had probably been one big joke to her all along.

Is that how she saw him, as one big joke?

Maybe she was right, maybe Dad had been right all along. Maybe he should just stay put, get a proper job, give up chasing his childhood dreams, and play it safe and get on with his life.

There was only one person he knew would understand. He hastily dialled Jake's number. He knew his best mate would understand, would tell him to go for it.

But then, Jake's ansaphone cut in.

"Hello, this is Jake's phone, please leave a message."

It was the worst timing, he'd really needed to speak to him.

He begun to wonder if perhaps his whole life had been a waste – everything he had ever dreamed about had been leading up to this moment, and with just a few harsh words, Lou had burst his bubble.

Feeling like a complete fool, he picked up the phone again and, with a heavy heart, left a message on the Exploration Society's voicemail, explaining that he was sorry, but he wouldn't be able to go.

Chapter 4

That night, Ryan slept fitfully. He dreamt that he was sitting in a cave with a family of Yetis chattering happily away together. The cave had everything a home would have, including a wide-screen TV on which they were watching the latest Bond movie.

The phone was ringing, and all the creatures were looking at Ryan, expecting him to answer it. He reached out his hand and picked up the receiver.

"Hello? Is this Ryan?" said a voice at the other end of the phone.

With a start, Ryan realised that the phone ringing hadn't been in his dream at all, and he struggled to sit up while looking at his bedside clock. It was 2.46am.

"Yes, yes, this is Ryan. Who is--?"

"Ryan, this is Des Armstrong."

Surely he must be dreaming after all. Ryan looked at the book beside his bed; *Bigfoot, the evidence, by D Armstrong.* OMG, Des Armstrong was the most eminent anthropologist in the world, and had been a hero of Ryan's since that very first camping trip.

"Hello? Ryan?"

"Yes, sorry, yes, wow … Mr Armstrong, it's an honour to meet you, I mean, speak to you, I mean …"

The caller chuckled.

"Call me Des! I'm sorry to call at this hour, but this is urgent. I heard you turned down the society's offer of a trip to Alaska to verify the claims of a Bigfoot sighting?"

Ryan looked at Lou, sleeping peacefully beside him.

"Yes, I had to," he whispered, "my girlfr—" .

But Des Armstrong cut him off mid-sentence.

"Look, I'll cut to the chase. The Bigfoot Exploration Society called me as soon as they picked up your voicemail. This isn't a wild goose chase, there's compelling evidence to suggest that these sightings are genuine.

After all your research, they're certain that you're the best man for the job, the only man for the job. They need you to fly to Alaska to back up the claims by finding Bigfoot and putting paid to all the rumours and speculation, once and for all."

He paused, as if deciding to continue. "I'm a member of the society Ryan, have been for years, but I can't go public and risk my reputation.

But you, dear boy, are at the beginning of your career, and no such damage will be caused to you as, forgive me for saying this, you are not so well-known in the world of anthropology.

Look, I'm in town and can be with you by 7.30am in the morning. Meet me at the Society's HQ and I'll explain more. But bring a packed bag, because if you decide to go you will need to move quickly. We need you to get there before winter really sets in and it's too late. We need you in Alaska within 24 hours."

Chapter 5

Twenty-four hours later Ryan found himself in a hotel in Alaska, awaiting the arrival of his best mate, Jake.

Ryan didn't have all the equipment he'd need for the trip, so he'd asked Jake to go to the flat he shared with Lou to pick up some stuff he could sell or trade in.

Lou had told him she'd had enough and was moving out. Great, talk about burning you're bridges.

He'd risked everything for this trip, but it'd be worth it, if only he could just hear the sound of the Bigfoot chattering again. And, if he got to see one? Tiny shivers went down his spine, just thinking about it.

So now Ryan was waiting for Jake to arrive, having managed to get the money together to buy the equipment that Ryan so desperately needed.

When he got back he'd have nothing left and no Lou, either. He put those thoughts out of his mind and focused on the task in hand. He had an expedition to plan and just days to plan it in, he'd better get busy.

Jake arrived a couple of days later. The weather was closing in and looked like it was about to take a turn for the worse. Ryan decided that they couldn't wait any longer – they had to get to the ghost town soon.

It had been hard enough to find a skipper to take them there, but even the one who did agree – for a price – wouldn't be foolish enough to sail there in bad conditions, so the following morning, the two friends set off in search of Bigfoot.

Left alone on the island (the skipper refused to even set foot in the place), Ryan and Jake set off to find shelter. The sky was thick with snow, and although the boys were equipped with extreme weather camping gear, they thought they'd probably fare better in a solid building.

As the snow began to fall, the search became more urgent. Thick, heavy snowflakes fell. Within a matter of minutes the already frozen ground was covered in a dense white blanket.

The dilapidated, abandoned buildings offered little protection against the elements, but just when they were about to give up and pitch the tent, they came across an old church which looked like it had weathered the years much better. Its roof was still intact, so they heaved open the wooden door and stepped inside.

The air was still, and despite the decades that had passed since it was last used, the church still carried the faint scent of long extinguished candles and incense.

The ceiling was high and they were able to build a small fire inside, with broken pieces of timber that lay around in the disused building.

They warmed their hands on the fire as the pot of water Jake had put on began to boil. Gratefully taking the cup of coffee Jake handed to him, Ryan made a decision.

"This weather is only going to get worse. If we wait too long, we'll miss our chance.

When I've finished this coffee, I'm going to head out. You stay here, and if I'm not back within 24 hours, radio for help, OK?"

Jake wanted to go with Ryan, but he was exhausted after the flight, and besides, one of them needed to stay at 'base camp' and keep the fire burning – after all, when Ryan returned he would need the heat to warm him up.

He sorted through the equipment he'd bought after selling Ryan's things, and handed him an old fashioned SLR camera. The temperatures were too low for a digital model to be reliable, so it was back to basics. He also gave him some portable sound recording equipment.

Ryan took a last sip of his coffee, pulled on a couple of extra layers of clothes, and pulled on his heavy backpack.

"I may be some time …" he joked, as he waved goodbye to Jake and walked out into the driving snow.

Chapter 6

When Jake awoke several hours later, daylight had faded and the fire was almost out. Pulling on a head torch, he grabbed some more wood from a splintered old pew and threw it on the fire, gently coaxing it back to life.

He looked around the church. Ryan's sleeping bag was still empty, which meant his friend was still outside in the wilderness.

Jake opened the heavy church door and was greeted by a blizzard – the wind howled and blew swathes of snow into the church. He closed it shut and leaned his back against it.

How would it be possible for Ryan to have survived in such a blizzard?

Jake spent a sleepless night, waiting for Ryan to come back. The minutes ticked by slowly and by morning he was sure he needed to call for help. Something had gone wrong and Ryan needed help, if it wasn't too late already.

Chapter 7

It took him a while to reach them, but he managed to call the local search and rescue teams using the radio, just like Ryan had shown him.

In a couple of hours, the search and rescue team arrived. It took them a few hours of searching, but eventually they found Ryan, lying unconscious and close to death in the snow, not too far from the church.

Jake felt terrible – if he'd only gone out to look for him the previous night he might have found him, and saved him from the severe hypothermia the medics told him Ryan had.

The blizzard eased up enough for Ryan to be evacuated by helicopter to the nearest hospital.

One of the search party gathered up Ryan's equipment, which had been lying a few feet from where he was found, and gave them to Jake before Ryan was airlifted to hospital.

Back on the mainland, Ryan slowly gained consciousness. He had frostbite on a couple of his fingers, but other than that, the doctors said that, physically, he was going to make a full recovery.

As he was leaving, the doctor took Jake to one side.

"We're not sure how this experience has affected his mind. He seems to be suffering from delusions, seems rather confused at times. He keeps talking about a family, how he needs to protect them, but as far as we can gather he has no known relatives."

Jake shook his head.

"No, he lost both his parents a few years ago, and he just broke up with his girlfriend. I'm the only one he'd consider to be family now."

The doctor patted Jake on the shoulder.

"He's going to need your support. Only time will tell if there is any lasting psychological damage from his ordeal."

Chapter 8

Back home, Ryan moved in with Jake.

Ryan was subdued, and often had nightmares where he would shout out things that Jake couldn't understand.

Over breakfast one day, he confessed, "I can't remember anything after stepping out of the church. If only I could remember what happened …"

Sometimes he'd wake from dozing in front of the TV and grab Jake's arm and tell him that he'd met Bigfoot, that the creature was even bigger than legend has it, and that far from being scary, Yetis were gentle beings.

Weeks passed, and slowly Ryan recovered.

His rantings became few and far between, until all he ever mentioned about that trip was his regret that he'd gone at all, because it had cost him everything – his girlfriend, his reputation, and even his furniture because what Jake hadn't sold, Lou had come back and taken.

The trip to Alaska had all but faded from Ryan's mind. He was still waiting for his hands to heal, but was at least up and walking about again. He finally felt well enough to unpack his bag, which had stood next to the front door since he'd arrived back home weeks before.

He grimaced as he pulled dirty socks from the bag, and then smiled as he felt the camera he had taken with him into the blizzard.

He remembered taking some photos of Jake on their travels, and he wanted to see if they'd survived the trip.

After everything Jake had done for him, it would be a nice gesture for Ryan to have the photos printed and put into a frame. It wasn't every day you get to travel to Alaska, in search of Bigfoot, after all.

Unlike a digital camera, the old-school 35mm film from the SLR had to be developed, so he dropped it off in town and headed off to browse the shelves of the local bookshop, while he waited for their 1 hour service.

Arriving home, Ryan opened the envelope, and slid the photos into his hand, careful not to put his fingers on the glossy surface.

He smiled to himself – there was Jake, leaning against a tree just as a branch broke, dumping snow all over him. And there was Jake again standing outside the church.

He put the pile of photos down on the table, and went to make a coffee before settling down with the photos for a closer look.

As he flipped through the photos, he saw something which made his jaw drop and his heart beat faster with excitement.

And suddenly, the memories that had eluded him for so many months came flooding back. He remembered it all!

Chapter 9

Once he'd calmed down, Ryan made a quick phone call and few days later, met up with Des Armstrong.

It was the first time he had seen him since the day he had left for Alaska, but when Ryan had told him he had something important to share, the famous anthropologist had dropped everything to come.

"Just tell me when and where, Ryan."

As Des went through the photographs, Ryan watched his face, enjoying seeing the same disbelief that must have been on his own face as he'd leafed through the shots.

Des looked at him.

"Do you realise what you have here, Ry? Proof. Proof that Bigfoot is real. This is huge!"

He held in his hands a photograph of Ryan, sitting cross-legged on the floor of a cave, and another of him giving a high five.

In every single photo, there was at least one other creature who, apart from the size and hairiness, was exactly like him.

"You did it, you actually found Bigfoot!"

Ryan recounted to Des the events as he remembered them. He had left the church and walked into the woods, but within minutes he was lost as the snow was coming down so heavily that he couldn't see more than a few inches in front of him.

He had tripped on a tree root, and before he could pick himself up again he had felt himself being lifted into the air and carried.

He must have passed out, because the next thing he remembered was waking up on the floor of a cave, with several hairy faces staring at him.

He had been rescued (although he didn't know that at the time) by a family of Bigfoot. The biggest one, whom he had assumed was the 'dad', had carried him back to the cave, and the other ones were varying in size, from another adult – he presumed the 'mom' – right down to a newborn baby.

"This changes everything - it's the biggest discovery this century. You'll be world famous when news of this breaks!" said Des.

Then he stopped for a moment and looked from the photographs to Ryan, asking the question that was on both their minds, without even speaking.

Ryan shook his head. "No, I can't make these public. Yetis or Bigfoots – whatever you want to call them – they're just like us. They have families, homes, and ordinary lives. They're so intelligent – who do you think took some of these photos? They saw me doing it once, and they just copied it after that.

If I release these photographs the whole town would be swarming with the press, and the Bigfoot would be scared off, captured, or most likely, killed, by trophy hunters."

In the end, Ryan shared his discovery with only a few people – Des, of course, and a handful of trusted members of the Bigfoot Exploration Society.

He'd wanted to tell Jake, but in the end he kept it to himself, knowing that the more people who knew, the greater the danger of someone else finding out.

He couldn't risk trusting the safety of the greatest discovery of the century with anyone, not even Jake.

Chapter 10

The Bigfoot Exploration Society pulled a few strings and Ryan was offered a job lecturing at one of the country's most prestigious colleges.

He would frequently disappear on mysterious trips abroad, when he and Des Armstrong would take off together, sometimes for weeks at a time.

One day he walked into the travel agent's office in Alaska. The young woman behind the desk had noticed his Bigfoot t-shirt right away.

"You're a Bigfoot believer?" she'd asked him.

"You'd better believe it," replied Ryan.

He smiled and reached out her hand to shake hers.

"I'm Ryan."

"Olivia."

"Some people say Bigfoot lives in the Rocky Mountains," said Olivia, "but you know something? I've always believed they're right here in Alaska."

"Really?" replied Ryan, "I've always believed the exact same thing."

"I always dreamed I'd see one, one day. Does that sound silly? But my mom always told me 'follow your dreams', so that's what I'm doing."

"You don't say? Mine too. I hope you don't mind me asking, but do you fancy grabbing a coffee sometime? I'd love to hear how you came to be so interested in Bigfoot."

"Funny you should ask that," said Olivia, "it all started on a camping trip with my dad, when I was a kid."

FOURTEEN

THE VOICE IN THE GRAVEYARD

Each night after work, Fred Thomas walked home. He walked through the business park, past the shops and right through the middle of a church graveyard.

Each night, as he walked through the gravestones with their strange inscriptions, such as:

"Thomas Mann, who was struck by lighting, whilst sheltering under a tree in this very graveyard, age 15.[1]"

"In memory of Elizabeth Dansby, age 27 years, who was fatally burned by Zephaniah Black's non-exploding burning oil,[2]"

Together with the more usual:

"Ed and Lil Smith, beloved parents and grandparents."

On the night when daylight savings ended and he hurried a little faster. It was the first time that Fred would have to walk through the graveyard after dark and he was feeling a little anxious.

Flashlight at the ready, he swung open the creaky metal gate to the graveyard and hastened along the path.

Half way across the graveyard, he heard a voice calling out from the dark.

"Turn me over!"

He looked in the direction of the voice, but he couldn't make out anything in the pitch dark. He tried to turn on the flashlight, but it slipped from his hand.

He began to run. He ran all the way home to his wife, and told her what had happened in the graveyard.

"Don't be so silly, there's nothing spooky in that graveyard. It must be your imagination."

The next night, armed with his trusty flashlight, Fred once again made his way home and through the graveyard.

Again, just as he was half way across the graveyard, he heard a voice calling out to him from the darkness.

"Turn me over," the voice insisted.

But Fred didn't stop to find out where the voice was coming from, instead he ran all the way home. When he arrived home panting, again, his wife laughed at him.

"It's just a graveyard, what is there to be afraid of?" she asked.

Fred was beginning to feel foolish. Perhaps he had been imagining things, after all.

The next night, armed with the biggest, brightest flashlight he could find, he set off home, across the graveyard.

Again, just as he was half way across, a voice called out through the darkness.

"Turn me over," it cried.

"Enough!" thought Fred. "I cannot live in fear all my life. I must know what this is."

Setting off across the graveyard, he made his way in the direction of the voice, which continued its request.

"Turn me over."

Fred climbed over the tombstones and pushed through low-hanging tree branches until finally he was in front of a huge church crypt, fenced off by rusty iron railings.

He climbed over the rusty railings and descended the stone steps leading to the crypt beyond.

The crypt door opened slowly, with a loud creak. Inside was a glowing barbecue stove, on top of which sat a juicy hamburger.

"Turn me over," came the voice again.

Reaching out, Fred grabbed the spatula and flipped the hamburger.

The voice spoke for the final time.

"Thank ..... you."

---

1. There is a tombstone with a similar inscription on Southampton Common.
2. True story - Ellen Shannon, age 26, was tragically killed by "non-explosive" lamp fluid. Her family used her headstone to publicly shame the company responsible, R.E Danforth, for this deadly case of false advertising.

FIFTEEN

THE FIRE GOD

The faces of a dozen kids were dimly lit in the camp fire, as they gathered around to hear Papa Bear's next camp fire story.

The smoke from the fire wafted its way upwards, high into the night sky.

The distant hooting of an owl, the crackle of the camp fire and the sound of happy kids eagerly stuffing melting marshmallows into their faces filled the air.

Just then, the wind direction changed and the smoke started wafting right into Papa Bear's face.

For a moment he tried to waft the smoke away with his hand, then, jumping up, Papa Bear shouted, "I am the Fire God!"

He edged his way around the fire circle, before finding another place to sit.

All the kids thought this was strange, but no-one wanted to be the first to ask him the question that was on everyone's lips.

Andy was the first one to pluck up the courage to say anything.

"Papa Bear, can I ask you a question?

"Of course, Andy."

"Why did you jump up and say that you're the Fire God?"

"Andy, that's a long story. Would you like me to tell you?"

Twelve eager heads nodded in the fire light.

"Alright then," said Papa Bear, "here's tonights story …"

Bryce was running but he wasn't going anywhere, the way people often do in dreams.

There were flames everywhere, but the more he tried to move, the closer the flames got, until he could literally feel them licking at his heels, and then —

Bryce opened his eyes and immediately regretted it, as the salty sweat from his forehead ran into them, stinging and causing him to blink rapidly before reaching for the eye drops the doctors had given him.

The little bottle was sitting on top of a pile of books and, as the liquid began to soothe the pain, he picked up one of the books and looked at the label on the front.

Price Martinez.

He sighed. Why did they keep spelling his name wrong? It was about the only thing he remembered from … before … but no matter how many times he told them it was wrong, they never corrected it.

He thought back to the hospital, the endless questions which he just couldn't answer. Except that one.

"What's your name, son?"

"Where have you come from?"

"Do you remember what happened?"

"Where are your parents? What are their names?"

It was only on his 7th day in hospital that his name came to him, and he croaked it out through his smoke-damaged throat.

"Price? Did you say Price? Good job, now what about your first name?"

It had taken a while for the nice (but slightly slow) police officer to understand that it *was* his first name, but when he had seen the way the officer had written it down, Bryce had shaken his head.

"Y".

The officer looked confused.

"Why what buddy?"

So Bryce had just let him spell it with an 'i' – it was easier than arguing, and all he wanted to do was sleep.

It had taken several weeks before the doctors said he was well enough to leave the hospital, and he'd been placed with foster parents, Luke and Erin, while efforts were made to find his family.

Despite the fact that he'd been pulled from a burning building, and everything around him had been on fire, Bryce's only injury had been from smoke inhalation.

His skin had been blackened, but once in the hospital they discovered it was only from soot. The hospital staff and fire crew were astonished to see that there were no burns anywhere on his body.

When his family didn't come forward, they had given him the surname 'Martinez', after the firefighter who had risked his life to pull him out of the flames.

And now here he was, in school. Everyone called him the miracle kid, but it had two meanings, depending on how it was said.

The nice kids and the curious kids said it in a "wow, you're actually a miracle" kind of way. The bullies said it in a "well, if it isn't the miracle kid" sneer, in a mocking kind of way.

That all changed in science class, though.

Bryce was having a rough day. The cough he'd had since the fire wouldn't go away. It had been particularly bad that morning, and now Mr Weller, the chemistry teacher, was telling him he couldn't take part in the lesson.

"It's for your own good Bryce, after what happened to you," Mr Weller had left the rest unsaid, but Bryce could see the Bunsen burners out on all the desks, so he knew exactly what he was getting at.

No matter how much Bryce tried to convince the teacher that the flames wouldn't bother him, he wouldn't change his mind. Instead, Bryce was made to sit in an adjoining classroom, while the the rest of his class enjoyed a hands-on lesson.

As he watched through the window, one of the bullies – Brian Jones – saw him looking and leaned over the burner, coughing and spluttering, pretending to be Bryce caught inside the burning building.

Bryce could feel the anger rising inside. As he watched the boy mimicking him, there was a whoosh, and the flame flared higher and higher.

Brian Jones screamed – and fell to the floor, clutching his face in his hands.

"That'll teach you to make fun of me," thought Bryce.

It was the calmest he had felt since he woke up in the hospital.

It turned out that Brian was fine, apart from having his eyebrows singed off by the flaming Bunsen burner, but big bully Brian suddenly found himself the target of all the other kids' jokes, which meant that Bryce was left in peace.

His teacher, Mr Weller, hadn't got off so lightly. He was suspended from teaching, while the incident was investigated by the Health and Safety committee.

That night, Bryce had his dream again. He was wearing white, and it was hot, the sun was beating down on him. There were other people there too, all dressed the same, but one of them in particular seemed to be very angry with him.

Then Bryce was running scared and shouting, saying that he was sorry, but the man who was angry at him was pointing his finger at Bryce, telling him it was too late, his booming voice echoing all around him. Bryce woke up, once again drenched in sweat.

A few weeks passed, and life seemed to settle down. The bullying stopped, mostly because the ringleader still had no eyebrows and he was keeping himself to himself, trying not to draw attention to his appearance.

Bryce's disturbing dreams continued, and they were always much the same – sometimes he'd be able to run and other times he couldn't move, but always the angry man, who seemed to be bigger and more powerful with every dream, was shouting at him, pointing his finger and telling Bryce it was too late.

Occasionally other words would filter through in his nightmare – a woman's voice crying, a hand reaching for him, and just lately he heard some new words …unforgivable, rules, broke, disrespect, out of control … but the dream always ended with the sensation of falling and Bryce waking up with a start.

One evening the family which Bryce was staying with had a barbecue. His foster Dad, Luke, had asked him beforehand if he was OK with being around the barbecue, because of the fire.

Bryce was getting fed up with people treating him like a kid.

"I'm fine, honestly. Thanks for asking but actually I quite like fire. I enjoy watching the flames, it calms me."

Luke sat down opposite him and looked at him with the same concern that pretty much every adult had used since he was found.

"Bryce, it's OK to be scared. I'd be scared of fire if I'd been through what you'd been through. It's not a sign of weakness."

Bryce was fighting hard not to get angry. He wished people would stop tiptoeing around him or treating him like a little kid.

"I'm out of here. If you want me, I'll be in my room," he said.

As he pushed past Luke he glared over at the grill in a surge of anger.

As he did so, the grill burst into life, its flames burning brightly and leaping high. The steaks sat on the grill, were charred in seconds.

Bryce was confused about what had just happened. He hadn't even touched the grill, only looked at it.

"What's happening?" he thought. "First the bunsen burner at school and now the barbecue grill. Surely it can't be a coincidence?"

His thoughts were interrupted by his foster Mom, Erin, yelling at her husband.

"Seriously Luke? What the heck? Do you realise how dangerous that was? You're lucky none of the kids were near the barbecue then."

Bryce went to his room, listening to his foster parents arguing, the party now cancelled.

As the school year drew to a close, there was one bright spot on the horizon. Bryce's entire class was going on a camping expedition.

The weather was set to be warm and dry, and Bryce was looking forward to spending some time away from the classroom.

They arrived at the campsite, and once their tents had been set up they were tasked with building a campfire.

The novelty of what had happened to him was wearing off – or maybe the class had been warned not to mention it – and this time nobody tried to stop him getting involved.

It was fun collecting the firewood, then helping to kindle the fire and watch as the flames licked upwards.

As the fire took hold, Bryce sat back and relaxed, enjoying the calming effect of the flames as they danced on their bed of sticks and wood.

He closed his eyes, and as he started to drift off he once again heard that booming voice from his dreams, but the words were becoming clearer.

"Never disrespect me … learn your lesson … dangerous, angry young man … banished to Earth."

His attention was caught by the whispering he could hear. As he opened his eyes he realised that all the other kids were looking at him, and those sitting further away were pointing at him and talking behind their hands.

Strange. Bryce wondered if maybe he'd been talking or saying something in his sleep. Why were they all looking at him?

He looked quizzically through the smoke at the other kids, his eyebrows raised in question, but he didn't get his answer until later that evening, when his mobile phone alerted him to a video that had been shared on social media.

He was lying in his tent, and had just trying to get to sleep when the familiar beep sounded, and the screen of his phone lit up.

He'd been tagged in a shared video of their evening - showing everyone sitting around the fire.

"Boring!" thought Bryce, but just as he was about to turn it off – after all, he'd been there so didn't need to watch it – the camera panned in on him, dozing off in the background.

He watched as silence fell on the group, and then sat upright in his sleeping bag, all thoughts of sleep gone. He couldn't believe what he was seeing.

All the smoke from the campfire was heading towards him, literally engulfing him, swirling around him in a grey cloud.

He tried to reason with himself that a breeze was blowing the smoke in his direction, but he couldn't take his eyes off the screen, as the smoke spiralled and snaked its way towards him, before ... no, it couldn't be.

He rewound the film and watched again, and there was no mistaking it. The smoke was steadily threading its way into Bryce's mouth, hovering in the air as he breathed out and then disappearing into his mouth as he inhaled again.

Suddenly an image appeared in his mind. It was like his dream, except that somehow he knew that this was real. It was something he'd been remembering all this time in his dreams.

The man was shouting at him again, and his mother - yes, he knew that the woman whom he had heard crying was his mother ... was pulling on his sleeve, begging him to apologise.

"Son, just say you're sorry. If you don't they'll banish you and you'll never see your home again."

Bryce lay back down on his sleeping bag, but never reached the floor of the tent.

Instead he felt himself falling, as if his body was moving down ... down through the earth, but when he opened his eyes, thinking the sensations would stop, he saw blue sky, and clouds, and sunshine, lots of sunshine.

He could feel the wind in his hair as he tumbled, the heat from the sun starting to burn, until he realised that it was no longer the sun on his skin but flames, lots and lots of flames, reaching for him, and in the distance, somewhere far above him, the sound of his mother calling for him.

The sensation of falling stopped with a jolt, but now the heat was almost unbearable as the flames came closer and closer. He began to beat them off, but instead of the tent walls he saw brick, and above him windows and a door. The whole building, wherever it was, was an inferno and yet, although he could feel the heat, Bryce wasn't burning.

Then he recognised the place – it was the building he had been rescued from by Martinez the firefighter. He had no idea how he had gotten back there, or what was happening, but as he beat at the flames with his hands he heard his mother's voice whispering to him.

"Control it, Bryce, learn to tame the fire."

Suddenly, he remembered. He remembered everything. It was all clear now.

He didn't come from here – from Earth – he was a God, the Fire God.

He'd been banished to earth because ... he tried hard to remember the details. He'd been banished because he was unruly, dangerous, even.

The other Gods had tried to warn him, but word got back to Zeus, the most powerful God of all. He'd warned him that unless he learned to control his anger, he would be sent away.

"You're a danger Bryce, a danger to us and to yourself. If you can't learn to control your temper, and the fire which your anger causes, you'll be sent to Earth where you'll have to learn or deal with the consequences."

His mother had begged Zeus.

"Please, he's just a young boy. I will teach him ..."

But Zeus had cut her off, one hand raised to silence her.

"Your son is no longer a child. He must learn that he is responsible for his own actions. He will be sent to Earth, where he will see how much damage fire can cause. When he realises that people get hurt, maybe he will see the error of his ways and learn to control himself."

But Bryce was not happy, and had stormed away, calling Zeus a fool which angered the mighty leader further.

"Do *not* disrespect me Bryce. Angry young men have no place here amongst the Gods. You need to learn your lesson and I fear that you will never do so until you see the damage your anger can cause.

Go. Go now. Our gates are closed to you until you repent and show me that you can return with your power under control."

Bryce had never been angrier and, as he strode away from his mother and from Zeus, he engulfed his entire body in flames – after all, he was a Fire God and the fire couldn't hurt him, but at least it kept everyone else away from him.

He'd stood there for a moment, consumed by the flames, yet not burning, feeling the full power of his anger.

Then, suddenly the ground had given way beneath him and he'd fallen, flames and all, down … down … down, until he had come to rest on the floor of a building.

His anger had been so great that, even throughout the fall, the flames had only grown bigger. Now they were taking hold of the building he'd fallen into.

He'd watched in horror as the walls burned, feeling the heat as the flames surrounded him, not scared for himself because fire couldn't hurt him, but because he'd seen the devastation that fire can cause on Earth.

He remembered the firefighter's hands under his arms, dragging him out of the building. The same firefighter who had suffered burns to his own hands to save the boy who'd started the fire through his own anger and pride.

Bryce felt ashamed. It all made sense now.

Because of him, big bully Brian Jones' eyebrows had been singed off, and Bryce shuddered as he thought how much worse it could have been.

Even his foster parents, who'd only tried to be kind to him, yet he'd caused their barbecue to explode into huge flames. It was only by luck that no-one was standing close to it at the time.

Again he heard his mother's voice, this time sounding urgent.

"Control it, Bryce. Learn to tame the fire."

He woke from the half-dreamlike state he'd been in and slowly unzipped the tent.

Bryce crept outside to where the campfire was still smouldering. He held out his hands and concentrated, watching in amazement as the flames grew slowly bigger. Wherever he directed his hands, the flames followed.

"Tame the fire," he remembered.

Holding on to this thought, he closed his eyes and quieted his mind. He pictured the trees around him, the calls of the birds and the smells of the forest. He pictured his home and how it felt when his mother smiled at him.

He allowed his mind to wander through his memories and smiled to himself. He finally focused on one memory above them all, of his mother turning to him and saying with a smile that melted his heart, "I love you, my son."

At last, he'd found the quiet place inside himself, the place where all was calm and stillness. It had always been there, just waiting for him to discover it.

Returning from this quiet place, he opened his eyes and motioned his hand towards the flames. Immediately the flames seemed to fade and reduce, to follow his bidding.

Bryce kept watching the flames, picturing the stillness and drawing on the stillness in his mind, until the fire had died down to a tiny whisper of a flame.

A sense of exhilaration thrilled through him. He'd done it. He'd finally learned to tame the flames.

He'd found the secret, it had been there all along. Tired but happy, Bryce crawled back into his tent.

As he drifted off to sleep, he heard the familiar voice of his mother, "You tamed the fire inside you, I always knew you could."

Just then, he felt his body rise towards the sky. It had been a long journey, but, at last, he was on his way back to his home amongst the Gods.

Papa Bear smiled and put another log on the camp fire.

"And that story," he said, "is why I stood up and shouted, "I am the Fire God."

"Because, whenever the camp fire smoke drifts towards you, who knows, perhaps you too might be a fire god?"

SIXTEEN

THE TEENY TINY WOMAN

Once upon a time there was a teeny-tiny woman who lived in a teeny-tiny house in a teeny-tiny village.

One day the teeny-tiny woman put on her teeny-tiny coat and her teeny-tiny hat and went out for a teeny-tiny walk.

She took teeny-tiny steps along the teeny-tiny street, until she reached the teeny-tiny churchyard.

Sitting on the corner of a teeny-tiny grave, she saw a teeny-tiny bone.

And the teeny-tiny woman said to herself, "this teeny-tiny bone will make me some tasty teeny-tiny stew for my teeny-tiny dinner."

So the teeny-tiny woman put the teeny-tiny bone in her teeny-tiny handbag and taking teeny-tiny steps, walked back down the teeny-tiny street to her teeny-tiny house.

She put the teeny-tiny bone inside her teeny-tiny cupboard, took out her teeny-tiny saucepan and put it onto her teeny-tiny hob, ready to cook some tasty teeny-tiny stew.

First, I need a teeny-tiny nap, said the teeny-tiny woman.

No sooner had she put her teeny-tiny head on to her teeny-tiny pillow than she heard a teeny-tiny voice saying "Give me my bone!".

At this the teeny-tiny woman was a teeny-tiny bit afraid, but thinking that she'd been having a teeny-tiny dream while she took her a teeny-tiny nap, she hid her head beneath the teeny-tiny bed sheets and went back to sleep.

Again a teeny-tiny voice from the cupboard, called out 'Give me my bone!"

Now the teeny-tiny woman was a teeny-tiny bit more frightened.

So she popped her head out from under the bed sheets and, in her loudest teeny-tiny voice, called out, "Take it!"

SEVENTEEN

IT WAS A DARK AND STORMY NIGHT

...

It was a dark and stormy night; the rain fell in torrents, except at intervals, when it was checked by a violent gust of wind.

I was driving across wide, open country - there were no houses around here. It had been miles since I'd passed through a small town, and it'd likely be miles to the next one.

"Just my luck to be out on a night like this."

I looked at the fuel gauge, I had just a few miles before I'd run out of fuel.

"I must find somewhere safe to shelter from the storm," I said to myself.

Peering out through the windscreen, I tried to make sense of the misty silhouettes through the darkness.

As I came over the next rise, I could see a shape rising up in the distance. Right here, seemingly in the middle of nowhere, was a barn.

With the sound of the wind howling and the rain lashing down, I was thankful to have found a safe haven to wait out the storm.

Pulling my raincoat over my head, I raced from the car to the barn and heaved open the door.

I leant against the door. I was safe, at last.

It was just at that moment that I heard it, 'bump, bump, bump."

I looked upwards and could not believe what I now saw.

Bumping down the ladder to the hayloft, was a coffin.

"Bump, bump, bump!"

I stood, frozen to the spot.

Slowly, but surely, the coffin bumped down the ladder, making its way towards my place by the barn door.

"Bump, bump, bump."

Looking to my right, I could see a door leading to a small workshop. I ran in and banged the door tightly shut behind me, throwing the bolt across the door.

"Bump, bump, bump," went the coffin, on the other side of the door.

I waited and prayed. Surely, I would be safe here?

"Crash!" The door to the workshop caved in and through the gap where the door had once stood, came the coffin.

"Bump, bump, bump!"

Terrified, I reached into my pockets, to find something, anything, that might stop the relentless onslaught of the coffin.

I grabbed the first thing my hand came across, it was a bottle of cough syrup.

Now the coffin was right in front of me.

In desperation I threw the cough syrup at the coffin. Immediately, the coffin stopped.

EIGHTEEN

THE GIRL IN THE WHITE DRESS

It was a stormy night and the rain was hammering down on my windshield.

I was driving along the US 70-A to Jamestown, and I was in a bit of a hurry.

The rain was lashing down outside and I was pleased to be safe and warm inside my car.

Just a few miles out of town, I rounded a bend and came up on the crossing of the overpass.

Out of the corner of my eye, I thought I saw something in the distance. It looked like a figure, standing in the rain.

"Surely, no-one in their right mind would come out on a night like this?" I thought to myself.

As I drew closer, I could see it was the figure of a young woman. She was standing there in a white dress, her hair and dress both wet through from the rain.

"What is she doing out on a night like this, and dressed in such a strange way?" I thought.

Instinctively, I applied pressure to the brakes, slowing the vehicle to pull up just next to her.

Winding the window down, I called out above the noise of the wind and rain, "Where you headed?"

"Jamestown," she replied.

"Then hop right on in, that's just where I'm headed."

She opened the back door of the car and slid silently in behind me.

"Where to?" I asked.

She gave me the street name and number and we pulled away from the kerb, moving swiftly towards the town. It would only take a few minutes to get her home.

"I'm Ted, what's your name?"

"Lydia," she replied.

"Nearly didn't see you standing there," I said.

"I'm just trying to get home, I've been out to a dance," she replied.

"It's a rough night to be out," I commented.

There was no reply from the girl in the back seat.

We drove on in silence.

It was a strange place for a dance I thought, there wasn't a building within a couple of miles from where I picked her up. But I figured perhaps she'd set out before the thunderclouds broke and the rain started.

I looked in my rear view mirror at her. Her wet hair fell in strands across her face, but it was easy to see she was very pretty.

She seemed distracted. She just sat there, looking down at her hands, sat in her lap.

"Nearly there," I said, as we rounded the corner to her street. Her home was sat back a little from the road.

"Nice place," I ventured.

I pulled in to the kerb at the address she'd given me. As the car came to a stop, I hopped out to open the door for her.

As I opened the door, I had to take a step back. The car was empty. All I could see were drops of rain on the car seat where someone had been sitting, just moments ago.

I looked around.

Had she somehow jumped out of the car whilst I'd been pulling to a stop?

Confused, I walked up to the door of the home and knocked. Perhaps she'd already gone inside. I had to check that she'd gotten home safe.

The door was opened by an elderly lady, somewhat surprised to find a stranger knocking at her door at this time of night.

"I'm sorry to bother you, has Lydia already come home? I picked her up by the overpass but I think she may have run off before I could open the door."

The woman looked confused for a moment, then I saw a tear form at the corner of her eye and a half smile form on her mouth.

She reached for a picture frame which sat nearby.

"Is this the young woman you picked up?" she asked.

"Yes, that's her."

"Lydia's my daughter." The old woman said. "She was on her way back from a dance when a drunk driver came around the overpass corner too fast. He hit her car straight on, she didn't stand a chance."

The old woman looked over at the calendar hanging from the wall.

"The accident happened exactly 23 years ago today."

"You're not the first one to pick her up from the bridge, and I don't suppose you'll be the last."

"I guess she's still trying to get home."

NINETEEN

ONE MORE THING

If you've enjoyed listening to this story or audiobook, please consider leaving a rating or review.

Made in United States
North Haven, CT
15 July 2023

39075189R00085